G R JORDAN

The Hunted Child

A Kirsten Stewart Thriller

First published by Carpetless Publishing 2021

First edition

ISBN: 978-1-914073-56-4

This book was professionally typeset on Reedsy. Find out more at reedsy.com

There is a passion for hunting, some-thing deeply implanted in the human breast.

CHARLES DICKENS

Contents

Foreword

This story is set in the areas of Inverness, Ullapool and the Isle of Lewis. Although incorporating known cities, towns and villages, note that all events, persons and specific places are fictional and not to be confused with actual buildings and structures which have been used as an inspirational canvas to tell a completely fictional story.

Acknowledgement

To Susan, Jean and Rosemary for your work in bringing this novel to completion, your time and effort is deeply appreciated.

Novels by G R Jordan

The Highlands and Islands Detective series (Crime)

1. Water's Edge
2. The Bothy
3. The Horror Weekend
4. The Small Ferry
5. Dead at Third Man
6. The Pirate Club
7. A Personal Agenda
8. A Just Punishment
9. The Numerous Deaths of Santa Claus
10. Our Gated Community
11. The Satchel
12. Culhwch Alpha
13. Fair Market Value
14. The Coach Bomber
15. The Culling at Singing Sands

Kirsten Stewart Thrillers (Thriller)

1. A Shot at Democracy
2. The Hunted Child
3. The Express Wishes of Mr MacIver

The Contessa Munroe Mysteries (Cozy Mystery)

1. Corpse Reviver
2. Frostbite
3. Cobra's Fang

The Patrick Smythe Series (Crime)

1. The Disappearance of Russell Hadleigh
2. The Graves of Calgary Bay
3. The Fairy Pools Gathering

Austerley & Kirkgordon Series (Fantasy)

1. Crescendo!
2. The Darkness at Dillingham
3. Dagon's Revenge
4. Ship of Doom

Supernatural and Elder Threat Assessment Agency (SETAA) Series (Fantasy)

1. Scarlett O'Meara: Beastmaster

Island Adventures Series (Cosy Fantasy Adventure)

1. Surface Tensions

Dark Wen Series (Horror Fantasy)

Chapter 1

Innocence stumbled along with the crowd, struggling to see beyond the shoulders of the people around her. At only twelve, she was not a tall child and with the sheer volume of people packed into the streets for the parade, it was difficult for her to make out anything except her immediate surroundings.

On the other side, a building that was only three or four stories high seemed to loom over her in the dark of the night sky. Brightly coloured lights were hanging from lamp post to lamp post, some static and penetrating the darkness, others providing a mesmerizing display which Innocence was forced to stop and watch. She wasn't panicked that her family were not around her; after all, her father had said that they should meet up in front of the supermarket if anything should happen. Many people had been kind to her, seeing her walking along and the general mood of the crowd was one of celebration.

Inverness was not a city known for its parades and unbeknown to Innocence, the current festival had been thought out over the last year as a way of generating much more hope and excitement within the town. Edinburgh had its Fringe Festival; in Shetland, they paraded with flaming torches along the street, but here in what many deemed as the capital of the highlands, there hadn't been a symbolic parade for the tourists to flock to.

Someone had said a life celebration. It was modern, fresh, and certainly in keeping with the current wave of political correctness. If you're celebrating life, you could celebrate anything, as had been pointed out in many a meeting, thereby allowing people to join for any reason whatsoever. Someone had asked if it would be too flippant and not have enough focus, but when it all came down to it, people just loved a good party.

The parade started in the city centre and wound its way out, over four miles of walking. There were floats filled with musicians and dancers, but the crowd was also encouraged to walk along with them, a feat that would make the parade unique. People were wearing garlands of all different sorts, indicating what they were celebrating.

To Innocence, the only thing she wanted to celebrate was Caledonian Thistle, the football team that her father took her to every Saturday when they were playing their home games. She'd been bitten by the bug and knew she would love to go and see the giants in the Scottish game such as Rangers or Celtic, or even travel further afield to the likes of the San Siro and Wembley. Innocence was delighted when she could stand up from her seat watching her team at the stadium on the edge of town. They'd passed it briefly and she had stood dancing at it, singing at the top of her voice, although no one was quite sure what she was doing. It hadn't been long after that that she'd lost the family, but they'd be in the crowd here, dancing around as well.

The parade was now back in the town and a woman handed her a bottle of water which she drank to parch the thirst that had built up. This had not been a problem, although it would be for her younger brother. No doubt, Mum was struggling with him on her shoulders.

As the street parade continued, Innocence felt the vibration of her mobile phone in her pocket and, taking it out, saw a message from her father. It seemed the family had to leave the parade and he was wanting Innocence to head back to the car park in front of the large supermarket. When they had met up, she and her older brother would be allowed back into the town, but her father wanted to know they were safe and together before he left them. It was a drag, but at the end of the day her father was right, as she knew finding her brother in this crowd again would be difficult.

Carefully, Innocence pushed against the wave of people that were walking through and made her way over the footbridge at the River Ness.

Pausing in the middle, she looked around at the lights of the town, hearing the thundering samba beats from a group of men on a float, loud music in the air, and savouring the smell of food from many stallholders on either side of the street. With a sigh, she turned and looked to cut up through several back alleys on her way back to the supermarket.

Her father always warned her about walking through the back alleys, especially at this time of night, but with the number of people in the town, Innocence thought people were unlikely to be lurking here. As she crossed the street to enter a back passage, she saw two men standing behind a car parked on a double yellow line at the side of the road. As she went to walk closer right into the passage, the two men moved together telling her she didn't want to go this way.

Looking at them, Innocence wasn't about to argue, and cut

off to the left away from them. What the men didn't realise was that if you went along a bit there was a back passage up behind one of the shops. Not a thoroughfare so to speak, but she could nip up there, past the refuse bins and right back into the passage the men had been guarding. Innocence did so, holding her nose as she smelled the rubbish that was awaiting collection sometime later in the week.

Continuing her walk along the dark passageway, she thought she would be hard to see in her black jeans and top, and she grinned, twirling her long black hair as she made her way along. As she came to the edge of the passageway, Innocence could hear people and she slowed up before carefully peering out through the opening. It was barely wide enough for her to get through and certainly any man or woman would struggle but Innocence was able to position her head as she went into the alleyway in front of her.

She almost gasped. In front of her, kneeling on the ground, was a man in a green parka. His face looked swollen as if it had been beaten and there was blood pouring from his mouth. On either side, he was being held by two larger gentlemen wearing black jackets. They looked strong to Innocence—the sort of people you see outside nightclubs, warding you away.

Before them was another man. He wore a smart suit and was taking off his large overcoat and handing it to a fourth man. Innocence wondered what was going on, but she was wise enough to remain in her little alcove, barely appearing around the corner.

The man who had taken his overcoat off was then handed something by one of the other men. Innocence could see it had a long point to the front of it. As the man raised it up in the darkness, she could make it out fully and realised it was

4

a gun with possibly a silencer on the front of it. She watched as the two men beside the man on the ground moved away to one side. She saw the individual on his knees begin to shake.

'I don't care about the money. The trouble with you, Johnny, is that you don't understand the meaning of loyalty. I thought I could come here tonight, convince you of it, make you understand the need for it, but I don't believe that you've changed.'

'I have,' said the man on his knees, sobbing through his words. 'I have changed. Don't. Don't. Mr. Collins, don't.'

'I gave you time, Johnny. That's what hurts. I was prepared to forgive. Do you understand that? I was prepared to let you come make amends, but you didn't. You turned around again and betrayed me. See these boys standing around me? They know what betrayal costs. Maybe you didn't. Maybe that was my failing, that I never explained the full price of what your actions could come to. I'm sorry, Johnny, it must come to this, but there needs to be made a point. You see Alan here? He's thinking of doing a similar thing. Alan needs to understand the price of disloyalty and you should look at it as a privilege. I normally just send people out to dispose of the rubbish. I don't usually take it out myself.'

'Please, don't. No!' cried the man on the ground. As his voice raised, one of the men from the side stepped in and hit him hard right in the face, silencing him.

'Well, it's not the time to talk it through now,' said the man with the gun. 'We'll raise too many suspicions. Too many people to hear you, especially now you're a blubbering wreck starting to lift your voice when I told you not to.'

'I'll be quiet,' said the man in a hushed whisper. Innocence could still see the tears coming from him. She wanted to step out and tell these people that this was wrong, but she was twelve, not five. She began to understand what was happening and was now looking on in horrid fascination. You saw this sort of thing in movies or books, but not here. She'd cut through this back alley many a time in her life. Just a little bit up, if you looked on the right-hand side, there was that funny poster of a clown. The shop it was in had gone bust, but the poster was still there. Many kids would walk past it, and stop and look. That was what you saw in these alleys. Not some man with a gun.

'This will make the point, Johnny. Make the point to people. Been too much disloyalty lately, but you'll be setting a good example.'

The next moments seemed to be in a blur for Innocence. She heard the gun fire, but not with a loud bang. Instead, with almost a quiet nonchalance. Then Johnny fell over, his head violently bursting and redecorating the ground around him. Innocence had never seen anybody die, not even an elderly relative pass away. She'd managed to grab the odd movie where people have been shot, but most of those tended to fall about, give a last moment, some dying speech. Johnny was never going to speak again. As she looked at his body, which even in the dark was obviously broken apart, Innocence could not help the involuntary scream that exploded from her mouth.

'What the hell?' shouted the man with the gun. For a brief moment, he turned, looking at Innocence. A shaft of moonlight lit up the man's face in a picture that Innocence felt would stay with her for life.

'Get her,' shouted the man. 'Get her.'

While Innocence was feeling a shock like she'd never felt before, there was also an instinct that kicked in. As soon as she saw what happened to poor Johnny, there was no way she could fight, no way she could prevent what had just happened, but she could flee.

She turned back down the smelly alley she'd come along, knowing that to follow her would be difficult. As she cut past the bends to the other alley, she heard something ping off the wall. Continuing to run, she realised somebody had shot at her. Breaking free of the alley, she entered the main road and panicked about what she would do next. A glance to the left saw the two men who had blocked the alleyway turning at something coming towards them. It would be the boss, the man who had shot the guy on the ground.

Innocence needed to get away, needed to get out of here. She looked left and right for a policeman, but there was none to be seen. The samba beat could be heard in the distance, and Innocence ran for the bridge across the River Ness. When she got onto it, there were people milling both ways, but she could hear behind her a commotion, people probably being shoved out of the way.

Being small, Innocence was able to negotiate her way past the legs of people running here and there. She thought that was maybe why no one had caught up with her by the time she got to the other side of the bridge. Here, the procession was in full swing. Although the samba beat was now coming from afar, there were plenty of other people packed together, dancing and playing music. Innocence cast a glance behind her and saw the bridge with people shouting and complaining and a group of men who were forcing their way past.

Without a lingering look, Innocence dove into the maelstrom that was the crowd and made her way right to the other side of it. The flow was incessant, and she continued to walk forward unable to see much around her. Shoulders were level with her head. She wondered if at any moment one of the men from the alleyway would just appear in front of her placing a hand on her, meaning to take her away, and maybe do to her what they'd done to Johnny. She was shaking now but she wasn't a stupid girl. She could think. This was the safest place for her, wasn't it? In amongst the crowd, they couldn't see her. She would stay here. Follow the samba beat.

Innocence sniffed, forcing back a tear. Maybe she could go to a policeman, find a policewoman but not with these people on her tail. What if they talked the policewoman out of it, told her she was one of theirs. Innocence wanted to be sick, the image of poor Johnny now lying on the ground coming to her. When she turned this way and that way, all she could see in front of her face was the image of the man with a gun, the moonlight acting like a stage light and highlighting the villain of the piece.

Chapter 2

Kirsten Stewart rolled over in her bed, swearing in her mind at the phone that was playing a happy tune. She remembered the music from a concert last summer. At the moment, it was the evilest sound in the world. She glanced up at the clock at her bedside. Who was calling at 3:00 a.m.? It had to be only one person, didn't it?

Throwing the covers back, Kirsten swung her legs out of the bed and sat up on the edge of it before grabbing the phone; she tried to look to see who it was, but she had no contacts in. She simply pressed the button already knowing who it would be.

'Kirsten, need you in. Inverness base straight away.'

'Urgent?' asked Kirsten.

'I need you now. I don't need you pretty; I just need you now.'

The terse voice was Anna Hunt, Kirsten's boss in the service that she worked for. It had been a few months since she'd finished her training and joined Anna Hunt's team, a group that investigated the crimes that were beyond what the police had scope to handle, those which required a more direct method of operation. Often, they would work in the dark, taking out threats that if handled in the normal way, would never be neutralised in time before significant events occurred. It hadn't been long since Kirsten had foiled an attempt on the First Minister's life, thus raising the profile of not only herself, but of Anna Hunt, who somehow managed to take credit for having her operative in the right place despite having sent numerous people to three incorrect locations.

'On my way,' said Kirsten, closing the call and placing the phone back on the sideboard beside her. Kirsten looked over at the photograph on the wall which showed her and her brother some three years before. The man was now in a home for those with severe dementia, and no longer knew his sister. Kirsten still visited him when able, a side of her life that just seemed to linger.

Kirsten's hair was a mess, but she wrapped it up as best she could in a ponytail behind her, and slid on her black jeans, black t-shirt, and leather jacket. Once her boots were on, she picked up her keys and made her way to her car before driving a short distance into the centre of Inverness and to a rather old house on a back street where the streetlights didn't all work for most of the year.

During the day, the downstairs had an office front that was used as cover for the service base. With it being night-time, Kirsten let herself in with a key, aware that many cameras were watching her entrance. Making her way to the rear of the ground floor, she took the stairs up to the highest floor before knocking on the door and opening to enter her own office. She was surprised to see her boss sitting casually swinging around in Kirsten's chair, but with a look of agitation on her face.

'Good, you're in,' said Anna Hunt, and stood up, looking immaculate as ever. There was a black jacket over the top of a crisp white blouse and a skirt that barely passed her knees, but which was not tight, meaning the woman could run in it if necessary. Anna tended to stay out of the action these days, but Kirsten was trained to notice the little things. The fact that she was wearing an outfit that you could break into a run in, meant that Anna was not simply someone who hung about the office making decisions.

In Kirsten's time with the service, that was all Kirsten had seen Anna do, but other people had spoken of her as being a heck of an operative back in the day. She was certainly efficient but Kirsten's level of trust in the woman was certainly not complete. The thing about this role was that it was one thing to trust people to do their job, another thing to trust them with your own life. They taught you that when you started out by taking you aside and saying to you, 'You are there to look after you. The service is there to use you.' In a place where you were taught to distrust the actions and motives of everyone you investigated, that mistrust seemed to linger around all your colleagues.

'Come with me; Justin's in the other room,' said Anna. 'I think he's beginning to find things.'

Kirsten followed, unaware of what Anna was even talking about. As she entered the small room across the landing, she saw Justin Chivers, the unit's resident computer expert. Kirsten entered the room and she saw the man's eyes first flick over Anna Hunt, and then onto herself. He was lecherous and leery, but he was an incredibly good operative. Kirsten reckoned that's why Anna let most of his looks go unchallenged.

He never made comments to Anna, but Kirsten was the brunt of the odd inappropriate gesture. He hadn't laid a finger on her yet. Kirsten knew that would be the turning point because she'd take that finger and bend it back until it snapped. Until then, she wasn't a hundred percent sure quite how to deal with him. He'd always been helpful with regards to the work, and at the moment, she needed to build up trust in someone, even if he did seem to be giving her trust because of how she looked.

'Kyle Collins,' said Anna Hunt, 'Know him?'

'Of course,' said Kirsten. 'One of the major drug operatives within the town. Rarely seen though.'

'Indeed,' said Anna Hunt, 'very rarely seen. We haven't been able to find Kyle for a long time, but he's on the move now.'

'Really?' Kirsten replied in surprise. 'I thought people like him never came out.'

'He's dropped the clanger this time. Rumour is he was teaching someone a lesson and had to teach it to him fast. Jonathan Kerr, someone who's been associated with Mr. Collins for quite a while, and a user, was found dead in an alleyway this evening.'

'In an alleyway? The carnival was going on. The whole celebration thing.'

'Indeed. Rumour has it Johnny Kerr was taken out by Mr. Collins. Shot dead by him.'

'Any witnesses?'

'One, or at least one rumoured to be. Everything's quite sketchy. The police have been involved looking for a missing girl going by the name of Innocence Waters, twelve-year-old, black hair. Justin here will furnish you with a photograph. Police have been out at the family home. Unfortunately, the son has also gone missing. He's twenty-one and an adult, and probably just out looking for his sister. As you can imagine, it's a bit of a mess. Trouble is with Mr. Collins involved, the chief inspector contacted the unit, and he wants us to take care of this.

'The rumour is the child saw Kyle Collins execute Johnny Kerr. If that's the case, she needs to be taken into protective custody. Word on the street is there's a criminal manhunt out for her and time's ticking. If it's true that she saw him execute someone, that's Kyle Collins into jail and not getting out for the rest of his life. The man's sixty, probably ready for his retirement. If the police nail him on this, he's gone forever.'

'Any idea where she went?' asked Kirsten.

'It seems she's bright. She disappeared down an alley, and then out into the carnival. There was certainly a lot of commotion. Some of Collins's men trying to get across the bridge over the River Ness, the footbridge. The carnival was passing by that way.'

'Smart kid,' said Kirsten. 'I read that the procession itself was going to be over a mile long. What height is she?'

'She's barely five feet,' said Justin Chivers.

'She stays in the middle of that,' said Kirsten, 'they're really going to struggle to see her. She can disappear away at any time, but it's where she goes next. Any idea what she was wearing?'

'Inverness Caledonian Thistle football top, black jeans, no jacket.'

'Not got a lot then to change into,' said Kirsten, 'so that will make it interesting. Anything on the internet, Justin?'

'I'm scanning her Facebook page. She's got Instagram. She's got the lot,' said Justin, 'but she's been quiet. It appears our girl really isn't stupid.'

'What sort of a person is she?'

'As far as I know,' said Anna, 'she's up at the top of the class, possibly quite determined.'

'Any chance she's going to rendezvous back to the house?'

'Her father told her that if she got lost, she was to meet in front of the supermarket down by the train station. The police have had people around there all night—nothing.'

'What time did this all kick off at?' asked Kirsten.

'Eight o'clock, half eight at night. We weren't involved until midnight. I didn't want to wake you until I got my own brief and realised what was happening. I need you to go and find that girl, bring her in. She's hot property, Kirsten. If he gets his hands on her, she's dead. Collins won't take the risk; he'll just kill her. For the police and everybody that's fighting against the scum like this, this girl's the ideal witness. She'll put him away.'

'What about the family?'

'They're under police protection, but they may be worth a look at,' said Anna. 'See if they know any of the haunts where she's likely to go.'

'Did she have any money on her?' asked Kirsten.

'She has a wallet, and she has an account. She took out £40 that night,' said Anna, 'but the card hasn't been used since.'

'What's the likelihood of Collins tracking that if she did use it?'

'Not great,' said Anna, 'but it depends. If he's got somebody inside, then he'd have a chance right away. She hasn't used it anyway.'

'What time's it now? Half-past three. If she's still out in the street, she could be wandering anywhere. Okay, I'll go and see the family. I'll just have a word with Justin here before I go.'

'I'll be down at the police station,' said Anna; 'need to have a chat about what's going on. I have a few other leads being pushed. To be honest, she's a twelve-year-old kid. I doubt she's going to contact too many people. If she does, Justin will be on top of it.'

'Don't worry. We're on it,' said Kirsten, but inside, she wasn't so hopeful. Looking for the twelve-year-old kid could be like a needle in a haystack. Where would she go? Would she run to friends or was she too clever for that? Would she take herself off into the hills or would she go back to the family? How much did she see? Rumour was only that—rumour. Would they find her and then realise that actually she hadn't seen anything? Anna was right. Kyle Collins would not take that chance. If he found her, the girl was dead.

Kirsten could feel the adrenaline rising through her, which was good because at half-past three in the morning, she was anything but bouncing. She poured herself a coffee, said farewell to Anna who was making her way down the stairs, and returned to the small office where Justin Chivers sat behind this computer.

'I pulled up a chair for you, right beside me,' said Justin. As Kirsten sat down, she clocked his glance at her.

'Eyes on screen. We've got work to do. If the last place they saw her was in the crowd just after the bridge, let's assume she's on foot and not grabbed any public transport. Assume she does four miles an hour. What's our radius for her?'

'You're probably looking about twenty-five miles, something like that. Although she would stick out on the roads. I think she's closer in than that.'

'A lot depends on the intelligence of the girl,' said Kirsten, 'I'll need to go and see her family. In the meantime, we also need to check what the police have been doing, contact taxi firms, any other modes of transport we can think of. Need you to get onto that, Justin. Also, scan through all her accounts.

15

Don't be afraid to go back into brothers, sisters, cousins. See if we can't find some place she could go and hide, especially if the brother's out on the loose; there's always the chance that he's picked her up. Do we know if he had a car?'

'Unknown,' says Justin. 'Nobody's told me, but then again, that not uncommon, is it?'

Kirsten ignored the comment, but it was true that at times Justin was not told a lot of things. As Anna Hunt once pointed out, that was due to the fact that Justin could talk. If you wanted something kept secret, he was not the man for it to be given to. Any good-looking woman would soon extract the information from him. A serious flaw, which Anna said she was going to have to work on.

'In that case, as I don't have many leads, I think I shall go and see the family. We need to start hunting possible locations. If Anna's down with the police, we should get some sightings, but it's all looking a bit like a needle in a haystack.'

As Kirsten got up from her chair, Justin glanced up and watched her walking towards the door of the room. Kirsten spun back around, 'Eyes on computer, you. You know why Anna doesn't trust you, don't you?'

'Why?' asked Justin.

'Because of those eyes of yours. She thinks any sweet-talking woman could come in here and take that information off you.'

'You certainly could,' said Justin, and Kirsten shook her head.

'You know that's your problem, don't you? You don't know where to be doing that stuff. This is not a place for it. People need to trust you in this building.' Kirsten saw the man's crestfallen expression. She thought for a moment about giving him some sort of consolation, but instead, she pointed at his computer screen. 'That's your job, get back onto it. Don't mope. I'll hear from you presently.' Kirsten spun around and made her way down the stairs and out into the Inverness night.

Chapter 3

Kirsten arrived at a modest house on a new estate on the edge of Inverness. She noted a number of police cars around and also a new BMW in the drive. A smaller Fiat was positioned beside the larger car, and she believed the family to be reasonably affluent. The house was one of those new ones, smart looking from the front, but when they said to you there were four bedrooms inside, you weren't quite sure how they all would fit in. Outside the house was a neat lawn with a number of potted plants located around the door.

Kirsten strode down the drive and pulled out her identification to the police officer standing at the front door. He nodded, advised that PC Linsey was inside with the family, and then turned back to his duty of watching the street.

The inside of the house was everything Kirsten didn't have as a child. Her mom had carried the family after the rapid disappearance of her father, and with the issues her brother had, the house never looked pristine. Rather, it was one hastily tidied up mess after another. But for all that, Kirsten had felt loved, and now, as she looked around the hallway at the many photographs of the family, she could feel the pain of a child being missing.

After knocking on the living room door, Kirsten stepped inside, introduced herself, and asked for PC Linsey. A middle-aged, brown-haired woman stood up, dressed in her uniform, and followed Kirsten into the hallway.

'How are they doing?' asked Kirsten. The woman's face dropped.

'How do you think they're doing? The mother is panicking like anything. I've just called the doctor because, frankly, she needs something to calm her down. The father's up to high dough, and the son's run off to try and find Innocence.'

'And they've no idea where he's gone? Have they tried his mobile phone?'

'They have, and we have, and here it is for you, but he's not answering.'

'Any idea where he went?' asked Kirsten.

'The assumption is he'd be going back into Inverness. If he's gone anywhere special, nobody's saying. Nobody knows, to be blunt. It's just been a mess here. Tears, panicked thoughts, all sorts of things like that. Trying to get them to think straight, think logically is difficult.'

'Is the girl's room upstairs?'

'Yes. I haven't found anything in it, but you're welcome to search,' said PC Linsey.

'Okay. I will do,' said Kirsten. 'Who have we got inside?'

'George is the father, and then there's Marion Waters. The son is Ollie. There's another son who's younger, I would say he's nine, called Gavin, and then there's Amy, who's just five.'

'It's a heck of a spread, isn't it?' said Kirsten.

'That's because Ollie and Innocence aren't theirs, or at least not George's. They married quite late. After Ollie and

Innocence were born to her first husband, the man passed on and apparently George and Marion found each other, and Ollie and Innocence came along for the ride. There's nothing in the family history to show that there were any problems at home, so it looks like Ollie's just gone out on a fool's errand to find her.'

'And we need to find him,' said Kirsten, 'because that's dangerous. If Kyle Collins's men get a hold of him, who knows what they'll do to him to try and find out where Innocence went.'

'Agreed, and I think DI Cairns would back you on that one.'

'Where is the DI at the moment?' asked Kirsten.

'He's just popped out.'

'Great,' said Kirsten. 'Why are they in the front room?'

'Because that's the living room,' said PC Linsey. 'Somewhere comfortable. It's what they're used to. Trying not to take them too far out of their norm.'

'It's not out of the realms of possibility that Collins would come here or try and affect them in some way. The front room's very exposed to the front street.'

'I'm not sure the DI would agree with you, but he'll be back soon.'

'Okay,' said Kirsten. 'I'm not one to step on everybody's toes. Just a bit of advice. I'll head upstairs.'

Kirsten made her way up a brown-carpeted stairway to find a first floor that had three bedrooms. She entered a room with a large double bed and an en suite at the far end and realised it was the parents' bedroom. After a quick look around, she could not find anything untoward. She then popped herself into what appeared to be a boy's bedroom. Two beds, one smart and clean, and the other quite messed up with a lot of toys around it, clearly where the boys slept despite the age difference.

The last room she went into had soft toys in one corner, but also boy band pictures over the walls. Kirsten picked up a journal, which she scanned through, but which didn't say much except that Innocence Waters didn't really think much of the boys in her year. There were a number of photographs around the room of different places, but Kirsten couldn't recognise where any of them were. Regardless, she started taking photographs, as these pictures were all around the headboard of Innocence Waters. Satisfied there wasn't anything more to glean, Kirsten made her way downstairs and again knocked the living room door before entering. Once again, she introduced herself and a man stepped forward, looking decidedly wary.

'George Waters, Innocence's father.' He said it with a hesitation and Kirsten saw the woman in the room look over.

'You are her father. You've always been a father to her since we got together.' There were tears streaming down the woman's face and Kirsten identified her as Marion, the mother of the family.

'It's okay,' said Kirsten. 'I get who everyone is. I'm really just here to ask a few questions. Kindly take a seat, George and Marion, over here. We'll keep away from the younger children.' Kirsten guided the couple to a sofa in the far corner of the room, where they sat down, but she saw George having difficulty looking at Marion. Instead, he gazed out of their front window. There was a pair of curtains that draped in from either side, but otherwise, the window was wide open to the street. Kirsten was nervous about this, but there was a police presence outside which hopefully should deter anyone from

21

coming up to the window. A real thought was that something might happen to the family, bringing Innocence out of hiding and heading back to the house, and that way Collins could pick her up.

'You've probably been over this a thousand times already,' said Kirsten, 'but is there anywhere you can think Innocence would go?'

'We've given the police all her friends' names and numbers, and they say they haven't seen her.'

Kirsten nodded to Marion as she said this, then looked over to PC Linsey, who also gave a nod.

'Ringing them every half hour to check, but there's nothing. They're all very well aware of what's happening and they're to ring in straightaway if they see or hear from Innocence.'

'I figured they're also being alerted in case anything else is going on?'

Kirsten was indicating to PC Linsey that they should be ringing in if anybody strange was hanging around their houses, as Collins may have been able to deduce who Innocence's friends were.

'All done,' said PC Linsey.

'Have you holidayed anywhere here recently?'

'No,' said George. 'We don't; we holiday well away from here.'

'Where?'

'Usually down towards Oban. There's a caravan park down there.'

'Already alerted, although it's a heck of a trek in the time we've had,' said PC Linsey.

'Indeed, it is, but George, Marion, is there anywhere that your daughter would go? Anywhere particular she likes to stand and look? A hidey-hole she likes to sit in?'

'Not really. I mean, she always enjoys the centre of town, more life than up here at home. That's why she was down at the carnival. She was really excited, being able to mix and move about. She said it was just so lively compared to what usually happened. She gets us to go down to the free concerts at Inver Park and that. I'm never interested, but she likes all the bands and stuff.'

Kirsten turned over to PC Linsey. 'Have you checked anywhere like that? Band locations, Steam Works in town, places where gigs and that happen? I know it's a long shot, but it's worth it.'

PC Linsey was taking down notes and said she'd pass it on to the inspector.

Kirsten stood up and started pacing around. She kept an eye out the window, because it really was troubling her at the moment.

'Ollie,' Kirsten said to Marion. 'What sort of a boy is he?'

'He's very caring. Especially about his sister. He cares for them all, but Innocence and he are close in a way that Gavin and Amy are.'

'But is he reckless?'

'No,' said Marion. 'He'll have an idea what he's doing. He'll be going through from place to place looking for her.'

'Is he in a car?'

'No,' said George. 'The two cars are outside, and he hasn't got one himself. He usually uses mine and Marion's if he's travelling about.'

'But he can drive?' asked Kirsten.

'Yes. Yes, he can drive.'

Kirsten turned to PC Linsey.

'Car hire soon as they open. Need to check. What time did he disappear last night?'

'It was after midnight, so he won't be hiring one until the morning.'

'Good point,' said Kirsten. 'Have you checked his friends? Any one of his friends who drive a car? I mean, he's not likely to nick one, is he?'

'No,' said Marion, almost bursting into tears. 'He's not that sort of a kid. He's looking for his sister. That's all.'

'I understand that,' said Kirsten, 'but if he did take one, we'd have a number plate if we know it's missing. Just makes things a lot easier to find them but find them I will. How much money does she have in the bank?'

George looked at Kirsten. 'Well, maybe a hundred, something like that.'

'Put some more in just in case she needs to be going anywhere.'

'What? You think she's just going to take off?' said George.

'Look, your daughter has just seen somebody getting his brains blown out. She's seen something so traumatic you have no idea what she can do. She's also on the run because they've come after her. If she's a smart cookie, she won't come up above ground. Unless she starts to use the cash point, she'll do it and move on quickly. Yes, put some more money in for her. That way she also knows that you're doing something. You might not be talking to her, but she'll feel a comfort from it.'

The last bit wasn't necessarily true, but Kirsten thought she should offer something to these people who were sitting there worrying their hearts out.

There came a call on the phone, and automatically George reached across and picked up the telephone by the window.

'George Waters. Who is it?'

Kirsten saw the man's face drop and instantly started to hunt around for another telephone. George put his hand over the receiver. 'It's someone called Collins. He said he's ready to do a deal.'

Kirsten made a motion with her hands indicating that George should keep talking. She could see the man listening to what was being said on the other side of the phone, and he gave the occasional, 'Uh-huh,' or 'Yes,' or 'That sounds okay.' As the conversation developed, Kirsten wondered what was going on. She stood in front of George Waters, her hands raised up, indicating she had no idea what the man was doing. His hand once again was placed over the receiver.

'He says he's wanting to give us £2 million for our silence—£2 million for my daughter. He says we can just leave the country, go somewhere.'

Kirsten's heart sunk. This didn't sound right. Albeit Collins would be desperate to clear his name, the one thing that would hang over him was the fact that Innocence Waters could at any time drop him in it. Simply paying the girl to clear off wouldn't do. He'd want to know for sure. After all, it was a murder rap and a cold-blooded one at that. The authorities would want him thrown to the wolves, ready to spend his rest of his life in prison. No, this didn't make sense.

George was still talking on the phone and there was a sense of relief on his face as he seemed to think he was getting somewhere with the kidnapper.

'He says he'll just come to the house. He said he'll drop the money. Someone will come, give us the money and we just go. That solves everything, doesn't it? We could just get out of here.'

PC Linsey was standing up and advising that this was not always the case. 'George, just keep the man talking.' She was calling in on her phone, seeing if she could get any trace on the call being made, and Kirsten was surprised that Collins was staying in the line this long. Of course, it wouldn't be Collins, it would be somebody else. Collins would never be so daft as to do this on his own. Plausible deniability. Somebody else did it on his behalf. Somebody else scamming them, but why bother calling up? Why even think of it? And then it hit Kirsten. The phone, by the window, at the street. As she looked out, she saw the car roll by. She took two steps, shouting at PC Linsey to get down, and threw herself at George Waters. She caught the man in the midriff, knocking him backwards to the floor, the phone flying out of his hand. Before she'd hit the floor, the front window shattered.

Chapter 4

Kirsten held George Waters on the ground, making sure he didn't try to get up again. She could feel the man's heart pounding as she landed with her head on his chest. There was glass all around them, but Kirsten was not concerned about that at this time. Instead, she turned her head back, shouting over to PC Linsey.

'Are you okay? Everyone okay?'

Marion Waters was shouting, screaming at the top of her voice and Kirsten caught a glance over at the two smaller kids, Gavin and Amy, who were cowering in the corner. Most of the glass had been contained at the edges of the room by the curtains, but in the centre of the room, the glass had blown across and Kirsten could see cuts on Marion and PC Linsey. The door of the living room flew open, and a constable burst in demanding if everyone was okay.

'I think so,' said Kirsten rising. 'Watch this man!' Kirsten made her way into the hallway and looked out of the front door. Outside, two police constables were hiding behind cars.

As Kirsten opened the door, she saw there was still a car there at the front of the house and spun herself back inside as a gunshot took out the light above the door. *Dear God,* she thought, *they're still there. They're still looking to shoot.* Crouching down, she bent around the door, drew her weapon, and fired at the tyres of the car. With two more shots, she peppered the sides of the car before throwing herself back inside the house. She heard a squeal of tyres. When she next peered out, the car had gone.

Kirsten moved out of the house, checking the area for the gunmen before putting her gun away and shouting over to the constables hiding behind the car. 'Get hold of some backup. Ambulance as well. We've got injured people inside.'

'Anyone get hit by the bullets?' asked the Constable.

'No,' said Kirsten, 'but there's glass everywhere. They're injured.'

She reached down for her phone and hit the instant dial to Anna Hunt.

'This is Anna.'

'Kirsten. They've taken pot shots at the family. Front windows blown out. I've driven them off, but we need a safe house now. These people are under attack.'

'Okay, I'll get Justin to send you through one. I want you to take them there. No ambulances.'

'You're going to need a doctor then or somebody else in the house. Somebody who knows how to look after people because they're a mess and you need to clear it with DI Cairns running this show.'

'I will do, but let's get them in your car.'

'No,' said Kirsten, 'Three-car stunt. We'll be ready in fifteen minutes.'

'Roger,' said Anna and put the phone down. The three-car stunt was where three identical cars would pull up in front of a house. Who knew how Anna would get that ready in fifteen minutes, but that was her job. Meanwhile, Kirsten secured the perimeter of the house and began to see neighbours coming out. She held up her hands, calling over some of the constables, 'Get these people back inside. Last thing we need is for people to be in the street in case anyone comes back.'

'Comes back?' said the constable. 'You don't seriously think they'll have another go.'

Kirsten didn't know what to think. This was unprecedented. People having a hit and run on the street of a housing estate in Inverness. It was crazy, but with what was on the line, who knew what Collins would do.

'Just get them back inside. The key thing here is that nobody else gets injured.'

Kirsten went to the end of the street before returning back inside the house. Inside, PC Linsey was fastening a piece of bandage around the hand of Marion Waters.

'It cut quite badly. She could do with going to hospital.'

'Ambulances are on their way, but then we're on the move. George, go upstairs, grab a suitcase, stick in clothes for you, your wife, and the two kids. You've got five minutes.' The man looked shocked. 'You heard me,' said Kirsten.

'But why? What are you doing with us?'

'You clearly aren't safe here. Your window's been blown in. We're going to get you to a hotel somewhere.'

This was a blatant lie, but Kirsten didn't want anyone to know that they were heading to a safe house. She got a call back from Anna Hunt and it took a full thirty minutes before three black cars arrived. George had been efficient in his packing and Kirsten ran out with two suitcases, throwing him into the boot of one of the cars. She then stood out in the street where the PCs ran the family into the middle car. Kirsten got into the passenger seat and gave a nod to the man behind the wheel to start driving.

Having established an Inverness base, the service had put various assets around the town, but Kirsten was still impressed by the efficiency which they turned up after thirty minutes to site and extracted the family. The cars peeled off and for the next two miles, constantly readjusted position, the middle car going to the front and the rear car into the middle again, before ending up at the front. As they reached the edge of Inverness, all three cars left in different directions.

'That's the car over the Kessock bridge.' Kirsten checked her rear-view mirror but was struggling to see anyone behind them who hadn't been there before. The car then pulled off and started driving through the Black Isle along tracks that most cars never see. Looking behind her again, there was no one. After taking another three or four different turns, the car arrived at a farmhouse located in the middle of the Black Isle.

Kirsten ushered the family out and the black car drove off to begin another load of snaking turns around the isle. Eventually all three black cars would join up again before going back to the base, but Kirsten opened the farmhouse door and ushered the family inside quickly. As they entered the kitchen, she heard George shout and Marion scream. Kirsten ran in, but there was a friendly face there. A white-haired woman, quite small, but of large build and a pleasing smile.

'George, Marion, this is Samantha. She's going to take care of you.'

'I'm sorry,' said George. 'This woman? But what is she going to do if they come with guns?'

'She's going to make sure they don't get anywhere near this building. She will have you somewhere safe and she will also eliminate most of the threat that comes at you. Samantha may not look like something but trust me, that's the whole point. In this business we keep our cards very close to our chest.

George shook his head, but Marion stepped forward to the woman, holding out her hand. 'I'm cut,' she said. 'It's sore, it feels like its ripping.'

'Window blew in at their home. Sam, I think you might need to do some stitches.'

'Okay,' said Sam. 'All of you downstairs. I've got the medical kit below.' She pointed over to the stairs that made their way up but had a door underneath them. On opening, there were concrete steps descending down to four different rooms. One looked like a living room except there were no windows. There were also two bedrooms and a shower and toilet facility. The rear of the living room had a small kitchenette and Sam switched the kettle on, telling everyone to settle in. She then disappeared upstairs, advising Kirsten she needed to close the place up.

The farmhouse from the outside looked like nothing, almost abandoned, and Kirsten thought it was a perfect disguise. From above, you wouldn't see anything, and the family would be safe underneath. How long you could keep them there was another matter. People started to go stir crazy, but at the moment, because they were on a hit list, they needed to be off the streets.

The phone rang in the living room and Kirsten picked it up. 'Hello?'

'This is Anna, how is the lone stead?'

Kirsten looked up to see Sam coming down the concrete steps into the living room. She gave Kirsten a nod. 'Yes, Anna, lone stead secure.'

'Good. I won't be out, and you'll be on the move soon. Tell

Sam it's going to be her and them for a while. Has she got provisions?'

'Are you all right, Sam—food and everything?'

'Yes, Kirsten. Tell Anna I'm fine. We can last at least a week to two weeks at the moment. I take it's nobody above surface?'

Kirsten nodded. 'Sam says, she's good to go. Says there's enough for a week.'

'If they're still there after a week,' said Anna, 'I'm moving them on somewhere, getting them out. It's too dangerous to be around close, but at least this will do for the minute.'

'I've got very little from the family. They don't seem to know where their son's gone at all. I checked the house, but I can't find anywhere that Innocence is going to go to. There's nothing glaring at me.'

'That's fine. Just check up on Justin, see what else he's got, but I need you back out here, Kirsten. We've got to find this girl, and quick.'

'You got anybody else on it?'

'We have half of the Inverness police force on it. I'm not looking for people to carry out a search, I'm looking for someone to dig into the situation, find out something that's for real, and then go and get her. You have no idea the heat that's coming on us about this one.'

'But we've only just got involved,' said Kirsten.

'No, the heat's not about what we're doing. The heat's about the fact that this girl can put that bastard away for years. If we lose her, there's going to be hell to pay.'

'Okay,' said Kirsten. 'I'll get up and get going. I think everyone here is okay. We've got some minor wounds, but I believe Sam can take care of it.'

After hanging up on Anna, Kirsten placed a phone call

through to Justin Chivers.

'Glad you called in. I've done a little bit of spade work looking at some of the photographs that are up online about her now that she's missing. Word seems to travel fast around Facebook and Instagram. There are words dropped here and there about where she might be, but none of them seem legit. I've continued doing a bit of work though. If you go into the history of some of the Facebook accounts, her brother seems to be friends with a guy who owns a boat out on Loch Ness. It might be worth a shout. It seems quite a distant connection, but I'm pretty convinced looking at the boat that the background's Loch Ness.'

'Where are the boats?' asked Kirsten.

'Well, the boat's about, what, quarter of the way down Loch Ness? But it isn't in the picture, so it could be anywhere up and down.'

'Got a detailed description of it?'

'No. I haven't,' said Justin. 'Just a picture, but she's a good-looking one, much like yourself.'

'Watch yourself. What does she look like?'

'White motor cruiser. I'd say she's about a six-berth, reasonably big. Got painters along the side, black and white. I'd put her in at about twenty feet.'

'Twenty feet, that's reasonable, isn't it?'

'Absolutely. The guy you're looking for has brown hair, about five foot ten. Reasonably well built. A bit of a pudge in his tummy.'

'Got a name?'

'Yes. His name's David Watson.'

'Brilliant. On it. I'll let you know how we go. You get anything else, text it through.'

'No problem. You know I'd do anything for you.' Kirsten put the phone down. It was time to go to work and she'd had enough of him, even though she'd been on the phone for only two minutes.

Chapter 5

The sun was bouncing off the rippling waters of Loch Ness as Kirsten drove along the road that hugged the loch, providing a view from almost every quarter. When she reached the Loch Ness Centre, a place where she'd taken her brother many times, Kirsten left the car and began to circulate amongst the public. With a photograph in her hand, she stopped people, asking if they'd seen Innocence or the boat she was reported to be on. Most people hadn't a clue when it came to boats; many pointed out boats that Kirsten could see on the water which were clearly not as she had described.

Undeterred, she pressed on and began canvassing around the village of Drumnadrochit. Kirsten made her way around the ruined castle grounds as well, showing her pictures. When she was approached by a security guard, she pulled out her credentials, and he was able to advise that no boats like that had been seen at the castle over the last three days. Kirsten felt a chill while walking around the ruins because it was there, during a case in the murder team, that a colleague had been placed up on a cross as a diversion for her detective inspector.

Memories of what she saw on the team still ran with her even though she suspected she may begin to see much worse now she was working with the service. The images still haunted her.

Kirsten continued south along the western side of Loch Ness until she found a small marina where she began to canvass some of the pilots of the various boats. She became excited when she realised that the boat had been seen only the previous day, motoring down the loch southbound. She quickly jumped in her car continuing along the road that took the tourists by the scenery of the Caledonian canal.

On either side, the mountains lifted up, tree-lined and in the sunshine. Kirsten remembered days of taking her brother there, days when he still knew her and they'd been able to laugh with each other. But on these changed days, that only brought more pain to her.

Inside, she was struggling having seen the family torn apart. Kirsten felt she understood what Marion Waters, the mother of Innocence must be going through. Like the way her brother had been ripped from her, so that he could never really have a meaningful conversation with Kirsten again, Marion had a child suddenly pulled from her. At least Kirsten had a warning, time to prepare well, for all the good that that did. Marion and George had none and they must have been in deep pain.

Every now and then as she made her way south along the side of Loch Ness, Kirsten would stop, take out her binoculars, and stand, scanning the loch. There were many boats out at this time, the Loch almost as busy as summer. Maybe it was the last twinkling of summer heading to autumn that brought them out. A last weekend to enjoy the countryside before the daily grind of work continued again. School holidays were complete and life was going back into that struggle through winter.

It was as these thoughts ran through Kirsten's head that she spotted a white motor cruiser on the far side of the loch. As she peered through her binoculars, she tried to focus and gauge the size of the boat. It was certainly about right, twenty feet with a white hull. And it was a motor cruiser. Kirsten sat down and pretended to be simply watching the loch, but every minute or so the binoculars would swing around and focus in on the boat.

A man was visible coming up on top of the deck. He seemed furtive to Kirsten, but he didn't stay on top for long before disappearing back down. For half an hour Kirsten sat watching. The boat sat in the water with only a gentle rocking motion. The only person to be seen on board was that man but then Kirsten could not see through the small windows that ran along the side of the boat.

Like most motor cruisers, the topmost part of the boat was reserved for piloting it. Kirsten had a clear view of the wheelhouse, but no one was up in that part of the deck. She imagined he would disappear down small steps and there would be a small kitchenette, a lounge, and bunks. Not a bad hideout and the location was good as well. The girl could have jumped on a bus or if her brother had got her, he could have certainly picked her up and driven down here.

The boat was at the end of a marina set aside from three other boats. On the east, there was plenty of activity, people moving back and forward, families taking shopping onboard. Beyond the marina, Kirsten could see a recreational building. Further still lay a large field of people sunbathing, playing football, and other family activities. She trained her binoculars towards the recreational building, then round onto the field.

She saw families and a young couple not worried about being

too overt with their relationship. She saw a dad with a kid on his shoulders laughing before bending down on his knees and pretending to be a horse. There was an older woman sorting out a picnic before handing it out to young kids. An elderly couple walked along, smiling in the sunshine, a Panama hat atop the man's head.

Everyone seemed like they were on an idyllic holiday, but then Kirsten saw two men sitting side by side. They wore dark trousers, shirts without ties, with jackets sitting beside them. They didn't seem to be engaging much in conversation. As Kirsten trained the binoculars on them, she realised that their focus was consistently on the marina. She watched as one man picked up a mobile phone and began to talk into it. She wasn't sure what he was saying but she could see him nodding.

Shortly after, another two men joined him, sitting down on the grass and watching the boat. Kirsten put her binoculars away, made for her car, and drove quickly around the bottom of the Loch before coming up to the turnoff for the parking area she'd seen. Once she was in the car park, she walked quickly and directly toward the marina before stopping on a bench that looked out onto the loch. Glancing over her shoulder, in the distance, she could see the four men still sitting, talking.

Kirsten was in a bit of a quandary. She couldn't say for definite that the girl was on board the vessel. In the distance, she had seen the man as he had come on deck, but it was too far away to confirm that it was either Ollie Waters or his friend, David Watson. Maybe the men were having the same trouble. The last thing Kirsten wanted to do was to head over to the vessel, drawing attention to it because if the men came, she'd have to try and outrun them in a boat that wasn't going to go that fast. They'd be trapped in Loch Ness with a very public shootout. Kirsten held her ground continuing to pretend she was enjoying the sunshine, but she didn't take her leather jacket off, making sure her weapon was out of sight under it, concealed between it and her top.

Kirsten saw the men get to their feet and walk along like a pack of wolves seeking their prey. One fanned out to the top end of the Marina, while the others headed closer towards it. They were far apart, and Kirsten was outgunned four to one if this was the right place. As one man walked along the pontoons towards the boat, Kirsten stood up and started to walk calmly towards the Marina. She heard a scream from the boat just as she passed by one of the men at the edge of the Marina. She could see the bulge at the back of his jeans where a gun was sitting inside, and Kirsten quickly removed it out as the man reached behind for it.

There was a momentary panic from him before Kirsten slammed the butt of the gun against the back of his head. The man dropped like a sack of potatoes. She saw the other two men at the far end of the marina pull out their weapons and she sprinted behind a nearby waste bin. There was a shot which disappeared somewhere above her head and Kirsten, pulling her own weapon, appeared quickly round before diving back in again. There was one man at the edge of the marina, and she tagged him with a shot to the leg. He was cursing loudly and there were screams from the general public at the noise the gun made. Kirsten was afraid that if the man at the front got inside the boat, he would put a bullet in Innocence.

Without thinking about herself, she took off from behind the bin, firing as she went, towards the man at the end of the Marina. She tagged him on his shoulder, and he flipped to one side. She ran towards the boat which was an uproar and she saw a youth fighting with the man before being joined by a friend. The butt of the man's gun struck the friend across the chin, and he fell backwards. Kirsten dived onto the boat, grabbed the man's shoulders and dragged him down. Her shoulder thundered into the deck, causing her to wince but she got to her feet, pulling the man and trying to force him over the edge. Instead, he caught her with an elbow straight to the chin and she fell backwards.

From a prone position she watched him pull out a gun and strike it again at the face of Ollie Waters. The man then disappeared inside the cabin. Kirsten followed him down, and then saw the man with a gun pointed at Innocence Waters's head. She knew the girl instantly from the photographs she'd seen, but this was a face that was terrified. Kirsten was also confused. Surely the man would've just shot her and left. Why was he taking her?

'Don't come any closer. I will drop her. I don't want to. She's worth more to me to have her alive. You understand me? I don't want to kill her, but don't give me no option.'

The area was tight and the man indicated that Kirsten should move as far back to one side as she could. Kirsten did so. Her gun held to one side ready to be used but also not pointing directly at the man.

'Okay, why? Why do you want her? Collins wants her dead. Why are you taking her?'

'He wants her dead. You want her alive? I want some money. We'll be in touch, but it won't be just for you. She'll go to the highest bidder. You understand?'

Kirsten nodded and realised the situation was about to get even more complicated. The man made his way backwards up the steps of the boat. When Kirsten followed, she saw him walking along the Marina joined by some of his colleagues. Two of them were in pain and she followed at a close distance. She saw them get into two separate cars in the car park.

She had managed to put a bullet into two of them and these two men got into one car. Clearly, they were struggling. Kirsten tried to memorise the number plate of the car but Innocence was taken by the man who had got on board and the other man that Kirsten had momentarily knocked out. As they drove off, Kirsten picked up her phone, calling Inverness police station, giving them the description of the car and the number plates. Putting her phone away, she turned to Ollie Waters who was standing in disbelief beside her.

'You wait for the police. People will come to take you somewhere to keep you safe. Your family's in hiding, Ollie. They were shot at; it's not safe you being out here.'

'They've just taken her. You've let them take her. She said what she saw. He'll kill her. You can't just let them go.'

That was the case, and Kirsten assured him she was getting right after them. Jumping into her car, she sped off but found it hard to pick up the track of the car she was looking for. When she suddenly passed a farmer's field and saw a car inside of the same colour, she turned around and drove back to it. The number plate was correct. She approached with her gun and checked all around it, but there was no one.

Racing back to her car, Kirsten jumped in and took a chance that they would be heading towards Inverness. She couldn't risk the child disappearing; otherwise, a bidding war would start, and there was no way the service could outbid someone with the financial clout of Kyle Collins.

Chapter 6

As she drove the car towards Inverness on the east side of Loch Ness, Kirsten made a call to Anna Hunt. Her boss was at the Inverness police station and quickly informed her that the police were searching everywhere for the car she called in. Kirsten advised the car had been found but no one was inside and quickly gave a description of the man who had kidnapped Innocence Waters. Anna Hunt said she would pass that description to all police cars in the area, and see if they could get a quick ID because if they didn't, they both knew they were in trouble.

As Kirsten reached Inverness, Anna Hunt called saying that there had been a possible sighting of two of the men in a car, heading out on the Ullapool road. The new car they were in was red. Kirsten put a foot to the floor, racing over the Kessock bridge, then carried on the A9 until she joined the Ullapool road.

The road was a single carriageway passing through the small village of Garve before heading over moorland to the west side of the country. Kirsten raced past the slower vehicles on the road but she couldn't find a red car anywhere. As she continued to pursue, she took a phone call from Anna Hunt.

They had identified two of the men from her description. Or at least, they'd had a pretty good guess at it, as Anna put it.

It seemed that Collins had put out a call for anyone to find Innocence Waters and bring her to him. It was a clever move. He hadn't told anyone to kill her because the call would undoubtedly bring out people not up to the task. The last thing Collins needed was a lot of murders attributed to his say so. Instead, he'd looked for the girl to be kidnapped and brought to him, meaning a lot of low lifes were searching for her. Anna Hunt reckoned that the two men were both Greek, the Tavares brothers. They'd also brought the other men as a backup for the effort. They were low-level and certainly did not have many connections, causing Kirsten to think they would go somewhere and hide low.

Kirsten continued her drive along the Ullapool road, but no doubt, the red car was travelling fast as well. When she reached Ullapool, she had neither sight nor sound of it. She called back in to Anna Hunt, advising that she was going to trawl for the next day around the area to see if she could locate the car or the Tavares brothers.

Kirsten bought herself some fish and chips and sat on the quay side at Ullapool. A part of her was watching people come and go, hoping to catch a glimpse of her targets shopping and buying supplies. Then again, that was unlikely. They would already have somewhere picked to hole up. In reality, she was feeding herself, unsure when she would get another chance.

As she sat looking out to the loch that ran inland from Ullapool, Kirsten could see the ferry for the Isle of Lewis coming into dock. The white superstructure with the red funnels made it stand out on what was becoming a sunny day.

Maybe they would catch the ferry, thought Kirsten. *They could*

43

make their way across the Minch. This was the body of water between the mainland and the Outer Hebrides, and the Isle of Lewis.

Standing beside a fence where the cars rolled onto the ferry, Kirsten nonchalantly watched as the ferry emptied before the next cars made their way on board. If the Tavares brothers were on board, Kirsten wasn't worried because they'd suddenly become trapped. She was also aware that her search might be useless because they could have changed the car by now.

It took about twenty minutes for the ferry to load but Kirsten saw no sign of the Tavares brothers. Satisfied that the ferry was going without them, she returned to her car and started to drive around the local area. There were a number of campsites to the north and to the south but Kirsten headed south first, visiting each in turn. As she headed back to the north, she made her way around Ullapool, driving through the streets over and over again, hoping for a sighting or a glimpse of the car.

When she popped into the supermarket that night to pick up a drink, she saw a red car in the far corner of the car park. After closer inspection, she realised it was the correct make and model for that spotted by the squad car back in Inverness. Kirsten made her way to the far side of the car park, sitting and waiting with her own drink. When the supermarket closed, and the other cars began to empty, she realised they must have abandoned it.

Making her way over to the car, she placed a tracker on the underside of it, just in case they returned on another day to pick it up. But this was a course of action that Kirsten doubted.

They would have picked another option. Had they gone to ground in cottage somewhere? Were they on a campsite or had they picked up another car and suddenly gone elsewhere? What if this was a decoy, a detour to throw off anyone following them? She would be stuffed.

Kirsten slept in her car that night, parked up on the edge of Ullapool. At 5:00 a.m., Kirsten started driving again, looking around. From her time on the Isle of Lewis as a police officer, she knew the ferry would be leaving Ullapool around about 10:30 a.m., but she'd be back to see people getting onboard.

Kirsten made her way to the north of Ullapool, visiting campsites. In each, she went to the owner, waking them and apologising profusely but showing her credentials. They understood how important her questions were. No one had seen a couple of Greeks, and as she reached the last one on the way up towards Lochinver, she had a bad feeling and realised that she'd need to turn back to check the ferry again.

The last campsite was basic in the extreme. When Kirsten drove up there, she contacted the farmhouse that ran the campsite. An older woman came to the door with a sharp face.

'What do you want?' she asked, offended that she had been disturbed.

'My name is Kirsten Stewart and I work for the government,' she said, holding up her credentials in front of her. The woman took them and studied.

'Well done you, love,' she said. 'What can I do for you?'

'I'm searching for miscreants in the area. A couple of Greek gentlemen.' Kirsten took out her phone and showed the photographs of the Tavares brothers sent to her by Anna Hunt. The woman looked carefully.

'Are these people dangerous?' she asked.

'Yes,' said Kirsten. 'Dangerous enough. They may have been

45

travelling with a twelve-year-old girl as well.'

'They were travelling along with a couple of women and a twelve-year-old girl, in a campervan.'

Kirsten struggled to contain the delight that was about to leap across her face. 'Are they still here?' Kirsten asked.

'No,' said the woman. 'They won't be here. I was talking to the women this morning. I didn't like them, you see. Quite loose if you understand me.'

'How do you mean?' asked Kirsten.

'They seem to be going with men that weren't theirs. I got the idea these people weren't married.'

'Why is that?' asked Kirsten.

'One of them was a black woman. You don't get that many around here and those two men were foreign. The other lass, she was Scottish. Probably Glasgow though, by the sound of her accent.'

Kirsten fought the racist implications that were being presented, keen to extract as much information from the woman rather than berate her backward attitude.

'You say one of the women was black. Can you tell me anything else about her?'

'She had that tight hair that they have. Not long. Curly, short tight curls. As big as me.'

The woman stood at five foot four, Kirsten reckoned. There was certainly no achievement to have reached that height.

'She was, well, all over one of the men, shall we say? I reckon she was one of them girls. Girls of the night. You know what I mean?'

'Did they arrive with the men?' asked Kirsten, a little bit surprised that you could find a call girl this far out of town.

'Yes. They came with them and they sent the girls over to

talk to me but I saw the men in the background. You said you were looking for Greek men. Yes, they looked Greek to me.'

'Did you hear them speak at all?'

'No, but they were very greasy. They're like that. They're definitely like that.'

'Are you sure it was them though?' asked Kirsten.

The woman looked up. 'We don't get people like that around here often. Summer, yes but not like that. I run a decent place. I don't like any monkey business.'

'You say there was a young girl with them?'

'I only heard her,' said the woman. 'I think she was in the back. Man told her to shut up several times. That's another reason I didn't like him. Look at the fields we have here. He could have let her out to play.'

'Were they noisy last night? asked Kirsten.

'No. Very quiet. Kept themselves to themselves in a lot of ways but the men with the girls. Yes, I think they were up to something.'

Kirsten was struggling with the image of a campervan with the Tavares brothers in and a couple of prostitutes along with the girl. Maybe the woman was reading it wrong. Maybe they were more sophisticated than that. The women were playing a part and maybe they were meant to look like a happy couple with a girl. But the fact that the girl didn't get out of the campervan and was only heard and not seen prompted Kirsten to feel that this was a lead worth checking. Even if the woman couldn't be sure that she had seen the Tavares brothers instead of, how had she had put it, 'a couple of Greeks'.

'Did they say or give any indication where they were heading?' asked Kirsten.

'No. Told me very little,' said the woman, 'but the campervan went off that way.'

'Do you have a registration for it?' asked Kirsten.

'No. You weren't here. If you had been here and told me to get one, I'd have got one for you but you weren't here, were you?'

Kirsten nodded and breathed deeply. The woman was annoying her, especially as Kirsten was so close to re-establishing the trail.

'What time did they leave?'

'Probably an hour ago. You might even have passed them. The women were doing the driving.'

Kirsten thought back to the last hour but she couldn't remember passing a campervan. But then again, she was in investigating other campsites so they could have passed on the road easily when she was doing that. 'You have no idea where they're going?' said Kirsten.

'I'm not a mind reader, now, am I?'

Check in time, thought Kirsten, *so 10:30 sailing on the ferry. They're going for the ferry.'*

'Thank you,' she said. 'What's the campervan look like again?'

'Big and white,' said the woman.

'Is that it? That's all you can tell me?'

'Had four wheels as well. It wasn't one of them six-wheeler ones.'

Kirsten thought it was pointless talking to the woman. She frankly seemed a little bit off edge.

'Thank you,' she said, and jumped into the car and drove as fast as she could back to Ullapool. Kirsten knew that the ferry would be departing shortly. As she reached Ullapool, she saw that the cars had already boarded the ferry and the rear of the vessel was being shut up. Kirsten ran to the desk in the terminal building, where a man looked at her wondering why she was sweating profusely.

'I need to be on that ferry.'

'I'm afraid boarding's closed. You needed to be here half an hour before sailing if you want on as a foot passenger.'

Kirsten slammed her identification down in front of the man. 'I need to be on that ferry.' He looked at the identification, looked back up at Kirsten and then got hold of his walkie talkie.

'Has it gone yet?' he asked someone, to which he got a, 'Just closing it up now.'

'You'll have to hold it. One more to get on.'

'No, it's gone. Master won't be happy about that.'

'Police,' said the man. 'It says here she's from police and she's asking to be on the ferry. Says it's an emergency.'

'Okay then. Let's just make it quick.'

The man pointed to the stairs. 'Up there, keep going.'

Kirsten knew where she was going. They'd built a new link to get onto the ferry, an extendable corridor that could move up and down with the tide so it would fit exactly with the side entrance where the passengers came on board. Kirsten ran as quick as she could and then saw a man in a red hat waving at her, telling her to get on board.

Kirsten entered the ferry, sweat dripping from her, and gazed around at a family seating area. She'd been here before. As the door closed behind her, she smiled to herself. *Got them trapped. Two and a half hours, Kirsten. Two and a half hours to put this to bed.*

Chapter 7

The ferry was full and as Kirsten began to walk around the deck, she watched faces looking back at her, but she saw no Greeks, nobody fitting the description of the Tavares brothers. She did see a couple of black women, but none had the tightly cropped hair as described by the campsite owner. Instead, their hair was long and black, curly, but it was past the shoulders.

Kirsten did her best to see if any of the hair looked like a wig, but it was difficult to tell. She couldn't really walk around accidentally putting her hand on everyone's head and pulling the hair to see if her wig appeared. There was also a white woman to be on the lookout for, but Kirsten could not describe her in any detail. After half an hour of walking around the vessel and not spotting anyone of note, Kirsten thought she should try the vehicle deck. First, she asked to see the master of the vessel and was taken up to the bridge where a rather perplexed gentleman in a white shirt with gold epaulets gave her a concerned look.

'Who exactly are you searching for?' he asked.

'Two men have kidnapped a girl, and there's also two women with them.'

'Are they dangerous?'

'They can be, but I have no guarantee they are actually on board. I believe they are, but we may also have others on board with them. I don't wish to alert them unduly. I'll make a call to make sure that in Stornoway, the police are aware as well. In one sense, sir, I've got them if they're on board. In another, it's a confined space and you have a lot of people on board with us. I want to play this coolly, make sure I can identify them. They may see reason and come quietly.'

'Well, I'm at your disposal for any help.'

'I'm going to go down to the car deck, have a search around if that is okay with you. I know by regulation, I shouldn't be there.'

'No, you shouldn't,' said the master, 'but these are exceptional circumstances, as long as you're happy to take the risk on your own, that's fine.'

'I certainly am.'

'But be careful,' he said. 'We've open deck at the rear of the vessel. Therefore, anyone on the higher decks, looking down to the rear of the vessel would be able to see you operating amongst the cars. I'd rather you didn't get seen.'

'That's understood,' said Kirsten. 'I'll do my best.' She looked out of the window and noted that the ferry was shortly leaving the confines of Loch Broom out into the Minch. 'What sort of a day is it today for the crossing?' she asked.

'Nothing excitable, pretty standard for the time of year,' said the captain. 'There was a wee bit of a swell on the way over, but I don't think we'll be throwing the crockery around.'

'Good,' said Kirsten.

'You'll be further down,' he said, 'so therefore you won't feel it as much.'

'That's good to know.'

Kirsten was taken downstairs by one of the crew and was led onto the car deck near to the front of the vessel. This part was closed in, but Kirsten could see that approximately the last fifth of the deck was exposed to the elements. For this reason, the vessel could take dangerous cargo on board, but it was giving her a problem if she was going to search the last number of vehicles. Kirsten made her way along, glancing inside every vehicle, but in truth, it was the camper vans that she wanted to get hold of.

She walked up to a number of them, listening intently for anyone inside, but she heard nothing. When she got to a white camper van, which looked to be four or five berth and with only four wheels as the campsite owner had said, Kirsten carefully checked it over. She couldn't see an alarm on it, and she managed to break in via the side door. Inside there were a number of sleeping bags scattered, and she could see up top, a bunk for two people. The place stunk and a whiskey bottle was sitting half discarded on the side. On the floor was a smaller sleeping bag, as well as another bunk where two people had lain. There were a number of magazines lying around.

Kirsten thought it rather bizarre that you would have a child with such pornographic material left lying. Checking the interior of the camper van she found nowhere hidden, no secret places. She suspected that this was the vehicle, but clearly, they'd got off somewhere, however they'd done it, but Kirsten continued to check the deck. After an hour, she returned up to the bridge to speak to the captain.

'They're here, somewhere on board, but I'm not sure where. Would you able to take me through the crew quarters as well?'

The master nodded. He personally escorted Kirsten around

each of the crew cabins. One by one, she searched through each of them, but there was nobody but the normal crew on board. She was taken through stores, through the engine rooms, every part of the vessel, but she couldn't find anyone. There was now only half an hour until they were into Stornoway. Kirsten placed a call to Anna Hunt who advised that the police were ready at the far end, and they would check every vehicle coming off.

'You sure it's not a decoy,' said Anna Hunt. 'Are you sure they didn't get off, get the vehicle on and then disappear? Maybe they're waylaying us if they're heading somewhere else.'

'Seems elaborate to me,' said Kirsten. 'They didn't know I'd found them.'

'Okay,' said Anna, 'if they're on board, we'll get them. I've asked the police in Stornoway to stop every car coming off, do a search of the vehicle, open it all up. If they're there, we'll get them.'

'Okay. I'm going to take one last scan around the vessel,' said Kirsten, 'just in case I'm missing anything, but then I'll be out front and coordinate with the police.'

Kirsten thanked the master and made her way around the vessel before taking herself outside onto the upper deck where she could see Stornoway coming into view. She spent a significant part of her police career here and had many times attended a ferry along with the dog handler checking for drugs being smuggled on board. Part of her was having fond memories of the place, but she had a job to focus on.

Once again, she scanned the area around her, but she couldn't see anyone. Getting back to the upper deck, she entered a narrow corridor from a door to the upper rear deck which led to stairs back down onto the main deck. As she walked along,

Kirsten bumped into a white woman with blonde hair.

'Sorry,' said Kirsten but then found herself being shoved through a door behind her to the men's toilets. It opened suddenly, causing her to trip backward and fall inside. A face appeared in front of her upside down.

'Remember me? About time I returned the favour.'

Kirsten was hit on the head with a butt of a gun causing the world to spin. She was not quite knocked out, but her arm was pulled backward, and she felt a handcuff being slapped on it. As her arm was dragged, she felt like it was going to be handcuffed to something else. Inside her, the blood began to pulse. If they strapped her arm up, she'd be trapped here. They could do anything to her. A hand flew up to her cheek and she saw another man's face, one of the Tavares brothers looking at her.

'Such a pity, a nice bit of stuff too.'

A rage built up inside Kirsten at the men's handling of her. She drove a knee upwards, suddenly catching him right between the legs. He grunted and fell down on top of her. She pulled at the arm being dragged behind her. Her arm became free and she grabbed the head of the man who'd just fallen on her.

Kirsten rolled over and plunged a fist down into the man, but from above her, her hair was grabbed, and she was hauled up to her feet before being spun around and thrown. Her shoulders took the main impact as she hit the wall of the restroom. Then the man followed it up by driving his shoulder into her stomach. Kirsten doubled up but managed to get her arms up in defence as the man started to throw punches at her.

In the mixed martial arts cage where she spent so many hours, it was not an uncommon occurrence to suddenly be taken by surprise. Minimizing the damage while she fought her way out had become second nature to her. She felt her arms blocking punch after punch. Then she jabbed forward several times, catching the man in the face. He stumbled back into his brother behind him, and Kirsten seized her advantage by running at them and driving her own shoulder into their midriff. The door had been closed to the corridor, so they clattered into it before Kirsten fought to catch a breath. She stepped forward again, throwing a punch to the man. He dodged it, grabbed her arm and again, drove her backward so she hit the rear wall.

The two men joined forces, trying to pummel her with punches. Again, she covered up, blocking time after time, the handcuff on her wrist jangling. When one or two did come through, she managed to ride the punch, but then she bent down, taking the beating. She felt one man grab her head and drive his knee up towards her face. Kirsten managed to get half a hand in front of it, but it still connected well. She fell to the ground.

'Now I've got you, you bitch,' said to the man, but another voice shouted at him.

'Not now. We need to go. It's docked. It's bloody well docked.'

Kirsten glanced out of one eye and saw the door of the bathroom being opened, the blonde-haired woman shouting at them. She fought to get to her feet but stumbled back again and felt another kick from the man to her face. As she lay there striving to get up, she heard them exit the room.

Turning over, she put her hands down, pushing up, but she was struggling. As she stood up, she felt herself tumbling towards the wall but managed to lock herself in a position to stay upright, as the handcuff swung on her wrist. Her face was bloody, but she made it over to the sink, ran the tap, and threw some water quickly on her face. She exited the bathroom and went out onto deck, where she saw that some of the vehicles had already started to leave.

There was a police checkpoint and Kirsten got hold of one of the crew members asking him to call the captain. The miscreants were on the move and his crew should be aware. She stayed looking off the front of the ferry but struggled to see the cars leaving, so made her way down to where the foot passengers were getting off. She watched how they were looking at her as she ran past, no doubt shocked by her bloodied appearance. She reached the end of the gangway down the newly built steps that led along the passage to the main terminal and saw a police officer she knew at the far end. Aidan had once been her partner and he was checking the foot passengers coming off.

'Kirsten, you look like crap.'

'No time, make sure you check everyone coming off here. We've got a black woman and a white woman with blonde hair with them as well as the Tavares brothers. Did you get the images?'

'Yes,' he said, 'but nobody's come this way, so far. The Sarge is out in the car park.'

Kirsten made her way out, wondering what a mess she must look like to everyone. She made her way across the car park. The sergeant quickly assessed her, seeing the handcuff dangling from her wrist. 'Stay back.'

'I'm Kirsten Stewart, the one that called it in,' and then an officer behind her shouted. 'That's Kirsten Stewart, Sarge. She worked with us before. She used to be here.' The sergeant straightened up, went towards her, and gave Kirsten help to stand properly. 'Are you doing it? Are you checking all the cars?'

'Everyone that's come off. It's taking time, but we stopped and searched them all.' Kirsten sat down on her backside sucking in air. 'Can I get you any help?' said the sergeant?'

'No,' said Kirsten. 'Just do it. Just do the search. That's all you need to do.'

For the next hour, after getting her handcuff removed, Kirsten sat watching the cars come off, but there were no Tavares brothers. There was no one of note. All the black women who left the ferry were interviewed. Their hair was checked to see if they were wearing a wig, but there was nothing and Kirsten didn't recognise them. Neither was the other blonde woman found who had bumped into her before shoving her into the men's toilets.

Two hours later, Kirsten was sitting in the harbour office talking to the sergeant, wondering what had gone wrong.

'And you checked every vehicle?'

'Yes,' said the sergeant. 'Opened the boot of them all.'

'What about the commercial vehicles?' asked Kirsten.

'Yes, we checked them. All still had their tags on.'

'I'm sorry?' queried Kirsten.

'The tags. When they close up a vehicle for transport, they put a tag on it. We checked it, we checked the paperwork, the same tag was on.'

'So, you didn't open and check inside?'

'No,' said the sergeant. 'We didn't need to. The tag read correctly.'

'But you can change paperwork and you can change the tag,' said Kirsten. 'I need a manifest of all the commercial vehicles that were on board.'

The sergeant nodded, got to his feet, and left the room. Kirsten could feel the sting from the punches that had connected with their head. She was battered and bruised but it was nothing to force her to stop working. It was nothing worse than a good pounding she would take in the MMA ring. But there was something else hurting her. *How on earth had they not checked the commercial vehicles?* She pounded a fist into the desk. 'Damn it,' she said. 'Damn it, damn it, damn it.' Now she'd have a whole island to search.

Chapter 8

Kirsten sat in the Balti House looking out towards the ferry terminal in Stornoway, dejected, but knowing she needed to eat. The missing kidnappers had disappeared in the back of a lorry which was later found with its rear door open and cargo still inside. The police on Lewis were shorthanded for a manhunt of this size, and they also didn't know where to look. The men could have gone anywhere in Lewis, especially if they had taken refuge with another party.

Kirsten spooned the large tomato that was sitting on her plate at the heart of her bhuna dish and chewed it several times while she pondered the next move. The police had been alerted and had asked for all their officers to put a watch out, but how daft would these people be? The other issue was they clearly were not there to kill the girl but rather to present her to the highest bidder.

The Tavares brothers were not killers, but they were certainly crooks and when Kirsten had spoken to Anna Hunt, her boss had not been in the most optimistic mood. The islands were small compared to the mainland but there were so many areas without houses, without anyone nearby. You could hide quite easily. There was also the possibility of being on a boat and because of that, Kirsten had tipped off the coastguard asking if they saw any unusual vessels anchored near the islands but again, that was a shot in the dark. For now, the girl had vanished along with the brothers and the two women, and possibly the next move would need to come from intelligence.

Kirsten spooned the last piece of curry into her mouth, swallowed it, and waved her hand at the man behind the counter. He came over, presented a bill that Kirsten paid straight away before leaving a small tip and making her way to the harbour to look out into the evening.

Sometimes in this job you had to stop. She had been on the run for so long tailing the Tavares brothers and before that, racing to find the girl before she disappeared. But without anywhere to go, without anywhere specific to look, Kirsten could just drive around this island for hours on end getting none the wiser. She would need something else before she would begin that fast-paced charge again.

She felt the vibration in her pocket and pulled out her mobile phone, putting it to her ear as she leaned against the metal rails at the edge of the harbour. The ferry was arriving again, slightly late due to the escapades that had happened earlier that day. The police had closed off part of the ferry while it travelled its repetitive course. The forensic team had checked around the men's toilets where Kirsten felt she had fought for her life, and had also managed to take off the camper van the Tavares brothers had come over in, but there was little to show for their efforts. The girl had been with them but little else was discovered. The trouble was everyone knew who had taken her; they just didn't know where they were going.

'It's Kirsten.'

'Anna. We've been listening to a bit of chatter and we reckon the Tavares brothers have a place near Callanish. Do you know it?'

Kirsten knew it well. She had worked here, and the Callanish Stones were one of the major tourist attractions on the island. There was a mysterious stone circle that no one was quite sure of its purpose, but it attracted visitors to the hill it was on for many years now. However, around Callanish, there were a large number of crofts and open land and if the brothers were hiding out around there, it was still a large area to cover.

'I am quite familiar with it,' said Kirsten, 'but is there any more detail? That's quite a large place. There is a number of outbuildings, ruins, caravans, things like that and the shore area is a myriad of lochs and rocks.'

'I narrowed it down from the island to one part of it. You're asking a lot, Kirsten, if you want an address.'

'Where did the tip come from?'

'We intercepted a call made to Kyle Collins from one of his men. It appears they're getting set up for a meet. The Tavares brothers wouldn't give their exact address, but they said they were in the Callanish area in Lewis so we're expecting Collins's men to make a move over there very soon. I alerted the police. They said they would keep a watch on the ferry but who knows if they'll come in from that route. The airport's alerted as well but they may use people we don't know. I don't think it will happen that quickly, but you'll need to be in the area just in case.'

'That's understood,' said Kirsten. 'I'm just going to watch the ferry dock and see if I can get eyes on anyone I know and then I'll make my way over. We got any more resources here to throw at this?'

'I'd rather use them in other ways,' said Anna. 'We got the police looking out and I've had a recent report that two men and a young girl were seen taking a bus over to Callanish so everything's pointing that way.'

'Anything more?'

'No. They got off the bus,' said Anna. 'That was it. The driver went on, didn't see what happened afterwards. The police have canvased part of the area but there's no houses where they were. They could have disappeared off themselves, they could have grabbed another car, any number of things, but it looks like Callanish is going to be the area for the meet. We've still got the phone line tapped so if any more communications come through, I'll tell you, but I don't think it's likely the Tavares brothers will be as sloppy as to just keep phoning the one number. They'll probably feed the information in via different routes. Collins is a smart lad as well so no one will know everything except him.'

'All understood,' said Kirsten. 'I'll check the ferry and then I'm off to Callanish.' As she closed the phone call, she grunted because it would mean a stop at the supermarket as well. There weren't that many shops on the west side of the island and most of them wouldn't be open towards the later hours of the night, so it would be better for her to stock up in case she didn't get back across to Stornoway for a day or two.

Kirsten spent the next hour watching the passengers come off the ferry and gazing at the cars as they exited out into Stornoway. She had a number of photofits of Collins's people on her phone but like Anna said, it was unlikely he was going to use any of the known ones. He probably paid for someone to come in from the point of view that if anything went wrong, he could deny all knowledge of working with them. He couldn't be seen killing someone. Certainly not again. He needed to keep everything as clean as possible in case it all went to court.

After a shopping trip, Kirsten made the trip over to Callanish, taking the road heading south initially before taking a right at Cameron Terrace. The road from there to Callanish went across moorland, which was long and sweeping, rising and falling, but with barely a tree in sight. There was the occasional clump of wood, clearly planted in an attempt to bring trees back to an island that once had been abundant with them, but a long time ago, the island had been cleared. To see a tree was certainly not a curiosity but was definitely rarer than on the mainland.

The night was overcast, but fortunately, there was no rain falling. As Kirsten arrived at Callanish, she initially took the car right to the visitor centre at the Callanish Stones. It seemed a strange place to meet, but as she made her way up to the monument, she realised the advantage of it.

The stones were at the top of a hill, with the visitor centre down below them. While you were amongst the circular collection, you could look out to the loch nearby, down to the road that Kirsten had come in on, and also off to the side where there were a few scattered houses. If the kidnappers didn't like what they saw arriving, they could always move away, rearrange the meet.

Kirsten stood leaning against one of the stones, pondering how she would do this. After surveying the land, she made her way back to the car and decided rather than sit and wait at the meeting point, which she didn't know was going to be in operation that night, she might do better to make her way around the ruins of the local area, see if anyone was hiding out in them. It was a shot in the dark, but it kept her busy rather than simply sitting in a car.

Working her way out from the Stones, Kirsten stopped her car and made her way out to one ruin after another. There was an old boat shed with a boat sitting inside, but no one had been there for years. The next one she went to was previously a blackhouse of some sort, buried into the ground, but there was no one there. Ruin after ruin was uninhabited. Then she came across one where a collection of sheep were inside. She made herself scarce before the light bleating brought out the farmer.

It was then she got down to a small ruin by the lochside. She noticed that some of the ground was trampled and there was a small path leading out to it. Slowly, she made her way in, from a different angle. In the dark, it was hard to see. Kirsten found herself hitting the occasional stone with her foot, and she bit her tongue not to swear out loud at the throbbing it had caused. The wind had picked up, and it whistled through the stone building in front of her, which only reached up to her own head. The roof was covered in grass but had probably been a thatch in its day, or covered in mud of some sort.

As she reached the corner, she realised it was an open door. The thought of shelter must have been quite hard if the wind was coming from the wrong direction. She drew her gun and slowly cocked her head around the corner, peering into the darkness. Her eyes were well-adjusted, but she could see no shadows. Flicking on the pen torch that she held in her other hand, there was no one inside, but in the corner, she saw a pair of rucksacks.

Carefully, Kirsten made her way over and began to unzip the rucksacks, finding food inside and a very small camping stove. She could smell the remnants of some sort of cooking, possibly beans. Then her torch caught the sight of a pan in the far corner. The red residue of the beans was still inside. Kirsten realised that things must be moving sooner rather than later, for the beans had not been cleaned out. Searching the rest of the rucksacks, she found mainly food. She discovered a small pail and some toilet roll. Otherwise, there was nothing of note. Certainly, there was nothing to indicate who owned any of these items.

Maybe they could trace it back to a supermarket. These days, there were cameras everywhere. If you could collect the food items, you might be able to get a time which these items were bought. It was a long shot, and Kirsten was not for sitting and categorizing the items. No, not when people were on the move. Slowly, she made her way back out of the room, retracing her steps to the car, where she sat inside and pondered her next move. Certainly, there was a likelihood the kidnappers had been here, but she doubted they were coming back. The items would have been hidden there, so they must be on the move.

The big question was, did they have a car, because if they did, the meet could be anywhere. If they were on foot, then the Callanish Stones was a possibility. It was less than an hour, but again, that was an hour of normal walking. How cooperative would the girl be? Would they have to carry her over their backs? If so, they'd be along roads, and passing people who would see them. Surely, they'd have a car with them.

Kirsten decided to make a move back to the main road that swept in through Callanish and park up just off it. Rather than sitting in her vehicle, she climbed out and took up a position in the grass, hidden from view by the dark night and her black clothing. As she felt the rain begin to fall, she realised she could be in for a very uneventful and wet evening. She pulled her arms around her because she'd had to jump on board the ferry without her own baggage and had only managed to secure some items quickly in Stornoway from the Fisherman's Cooperative in the town. She was glad that one of these items had been a large waterproof jacket. As she sat with it wrapped around her, she felt the vibration of the phone in her pocket again.

'Kirsten.'

'It sounds like things have gone wrong in this side.'

'How do you mean have gone wrong?'

'The father has gone missing from the house, the brother too.'

'What happened to Sam? I thought she was looking after them.'

'She was doing. Father and son said they were going for a sleep. Everyone was down below, but she said they were a clever pair, knocked the alarms off and disappeared out. The mother kept going back and forward to the room, telling Sam she was checking up to make sure her boy was sleeping okay. The pair of them were gone the whole time.'

'Could they be here?' asked Kirsten.

'I checked the ferries, and you were there too, so we doubt they came off there. So, I checked flights. They may have arrived at Stornoway on the late evening plane. I'm not sure what's going on, Kirsten, but you've got to consider these two are rogue now. They may be contacting Collins after them speaking before. They could do anything. They must be terrified.'

'Understood,' said Kirsten. 'I think it's happening tonight. I found where I believe that the Tavares brothers were staying. It's an old ruin, and they've left it. If they're in a car, they could be meeting anywhere. I'm stuck on the roadside in Callanish, hoping I'll pick something out. If I get anything, Anna, I'll be straight on to you, but I think we're clutching at straws at the moment. Did Sam question the mother? Did Marion know anything?' asked Kirsten

'These two are quite cute,' said Anna. 'The mother knew nothing. They wouldn't say anything, but I reckon they could be off for a meet. Whether or not they even had that information at that point, I don't know, because there were no phone calls going out. I reckon they escaped then probably tried to make contact. I don't need to tell you, Kirsten, you need to get on top of this. If those guys turn up, they could end up dead as well.'

'It's all understood, but I'm out in the dark here, Anna. You get that, don't you?'

'Well, find a better light then. It's what we pay you for.'

Chapter 9

The rain was steady and heavy, and Kirsten could feel the chill about to come into her bones. She wanted to shift position, but at the moment, she was incognito in the grass. A number of cars had come past in the hours during which she had waited. All had continued into the Callanish village, and she saw them stopping at houses with lights already on, so decided not to pay them any further attention. As the hour got towards two in the morning, the traffic had ceased. It was only the occasional police car going past giving her evening any highlights.

Kirsten had learned the subtle art of being a sentry. The old routine when you were given a watching duty, but through the middle of the night, you would let your body start to drift off but keep the senses alert. As soon as anything happened, the eyes flew open. The ears were the key of it, hearing things, picking up the sounds before alerting the eyes to be on the lookout. She heard the car coming long before it reached her.

The car headlights were bright. Kirsten watched the black tarmac suddenly light up with the rain gleaming as it fell in front of the headlight. The car was slowing as it came to the turn-off for the Callanish Stones and Kirsten primed herself.

It was difficult with such a bright light to see inside the car. She looked away from the beam trying to maintain that night vision that comes when the sun descends and all the lights have been switched off. Her eyes had adjusted over the time she'd been there, but she didn't want them to revert simply because of a car beam.

She could see two figures inside the car, a map being held up. Then the car made its way down towards the Callanish Stones visitor centre. Kirsten got into her own car and kept her headlights switched off. She minimised the internal lights as much as she could and drove at a distance behind the car, stopping well short of the visitor centre, keen not to alert them as they pulled into the car park. Kirsten jumped out of her car and made her way along the roadside. The rain was now coming down hard.

As she got to the visitor centre car park, she could see two men getting out but it was hard to make the figures out through the rain. They made their way up towards the visitor's centre as she reached the car park. She saw them then take the path up towards the Callanish Stones.

Kirsten skirted the hillside, keeping low in the grass, and climbed up from the far side. As she approached the hilltop, she realised how dark the night was, for the figures that she saw amongst the stones were mere shadows. She crawled closer through the grass keeping herself on the slope just off the stone circle.

'That's far enough,' a sharp voice said. 'You can stay there. The other buyers are on the far side.'

Buyer? thought Kirsten. *Is this going to be an auction?*

'I need to see her. I need to see my daughter.'

'She's here but first we need to know there's no guns.' Kirsten watched a man step forward. He frisked the party on her left-hand side. He then made his way over to the father who had spoken, rubbing his hands down the side of the man as well.

'Good. This is how it works, so make sure you don't step out of line because if you do, we are armed. You'll start to bid. The representatives of Mr. Collins state theirs first, then we'll come to you, Mr. Waters. Back and forward until somebody cannot raise the money, and I hope you brought the money with you.'

Kirsten wondered how the Waters family would raise money. Were they rich? Not according to her, but they did have large family connections. She remembered something about that. Maybe there was someone in the background, but they'd also have to get the cash in quick.

'I have the means to transfer it,' said Waters.

'Well, that'll be an extra 10% on top,' said one of the brothers. 'But let's not get over-excited yet. You haven't won the auction.'

With that, he turned to his brother. He pulled a girl out from behind one of the stones, and then dragged her forward. He stayed equidistant from the Waters family and from Collins's representatives. Kirsten watched. She clocked two representatives from Collins and then there was Mr. Waters and his son. Something didn't sit right with her.

There was no way Collins's people would do this. Let the Tavares brothers stand there without guns? Why not just come in and shoot people if Collins was that desperate? There'd be a backup plan in all of this.

Kirsten started to scan around the stones. Carefully she began to circumvent the monument keeping on the slope so she couldn't be seen. She suddenly froze as across from her view she could see someone behind one of the stones.

'Shall we start?' asked one of the Tavares brothers. 'Starting with you, Mr. Collins's representatives.'

'I'll give you twenty thousand for—'

The Tavares brother spat on the ground and grabbed the girl by the hair. 'Twenty thousand? I'll jump in a car and take her down the police station, let her squawk.'

'We'll give you fifty,' said Mr. Waters.

'Gentlemen, unless we're talking half a million, we're getting in a car.'

'Half a million you have,' said Collins's representative.

'Seven hundred and fifty thousand,' said Mr. Waters. 'I'll double it if you need to.'

'Two million,' said Collins's representative.

'Do we really have that sort of money?' asked the Tavares brother.

'There's a lot riding in this one,' said the representative of Collins. 'Is it a deal or not?'

'I will get you more,' said Mr. Waters. 'I will get you a lot more.'

'It's not here. Is it? Sorry, she's a lovely kid, but there you go.' With that, Tavares shoved Innocence Waters towards Collins's representatives. 'Let's go do business, gentlemen. I need my money now.'

Two million was a steep amount for Collins, even with the stakes that were at play. Kirsten's hand moved to her gun. She saw the figure, who was hiding behind one of the stones, step out with his gun raised. From her prone position, Kirsten raised her own gun and fired. There was a dull quiet thud and she hit her target, the man spinning, but not before a shot came her way that reverberated around the stones. Kirsten was unsure where they had gone, as everyone started to scream

71

and run.

Kirsten could see the two men from Collins suddenly run forward, trying to grab Innocence, but one of the Tavares brothers stepped in front and landed a punch on one of them. Mr. Waters moved forward. The other Tavares brother pulled his gun out, pointing it at the man. Kirsten knew she couldn't take the risk. One of the Tavares brothers fell to the ground as the other turned to fire back at her. A second shot from Kirsten caught him in the shoulder and he fell to the ground as well.

Collins's representatives went to make a grab for the girl, but Kirsten tagged one of them and the other started to run towards her. He made his way for cover, hiding behind one of the stones. As he came out the other side, Kirsten could see him pointing something at her. Innocence, unlike her father, seemed to have her head together and ran for her brother. The father was screaming, but Kirsten had no time to watch. As she heard a shot ring out just above her, she rolled to her right, getting behind another of the stones, knowing that the man still had a gun pointed at her.

She saw the Waters family running out of the stone circle and the man turned towards them. Kirsten fired, causing him to hide again. She needed to give them covering fire. Collins's representatives wouldn't care if the girl was dead, the family too. They just needed their silence. Kirsten couldn't see the man from behind the stone so she stepped out looking left and right, desperate to know where he was.

The family were just reaching the top of the path that led down to the visitor centre car park and Kirsten knew she had to protect them. Taking a risk, she stepped over to behind one of the rocks and saw the man with a gun pointed at the Waters family. She fired at him. Kirsten missed, but she'd caused him to duck back, missing a shot at the family. Seeing them start to run down the path, he then began to run that way himself, his gun pointed towards Kirsten firing a couple of shots that direction.

She crouched down tight before spinning out from behind the rock to see the man making his way towards the top of the path. With one shot, she caught him in the shoulder, but he managed to keep going. A second shot, she believed, hit him somewhere around the back and he fell to the ground. Kirsten quickly made her way over some of the prone bodies on the ground, hearing the pain and agony from some of the figures.

She saw guns and kicked them clear before finding the last man she had shot and tossed his weapon aside as well. As she looked down at the car park, she saw the Waters's car come to life, the headlights on. Kirsten ran hard down the path and cut off to the side on a quicker route to the car park. She had to run through bramble and long grass, and despite taking a tumble, she managed to roll back up, hurdle a fence, and enter the car park.

Just as the car was pulling away, she ran to the gate at the entrance, waving her arms desperately as the car sped towards her. She even pulled her gun and pointed it at them, although she had no intentions of firing. But the car kept coming closer and closer with no sign of slowing down. Kirsten threw herself to one side and the car disappeared off. Holstering her gun, she ran hard up the road as the rain came down. She grabbed her phone as she ran, dialling in for Anna Hunt.

'Richard here. Anna is indisposed. What is it?'

'Richard, it's Kirsten. I'm on the run. The family have the girl. The family have her. I've got potentially a couple dead up at the Callanish Stones who I've shot, but there's live weapons although I've kicked them clear. Police need to be aware as they turn up because no doubt the phone calls will be going in. I'm on the trail. I could do with the police out here stopping cars as well. I don't think the family's that clever. The other problem is if there's anybody else out here, Collins had men up here for a meet. I doubt they're going to work alone. I'm just getting into my car to pursue the Waters family. I'll try and get to them first.'

'What direction are they going?' asked Richard.

'We've just come from Callanish. They're heading out to the main road. Who the hell knows where they'll go after that? If I can get hold of the family, I'll go to ground with them. I'm not risking bringing them in via police so we'll need to sort something.'

'I'll keep Anna advised,' said Richard. 'We'll try and prep up some people as well. I think she's going to be busy for the next while.'

'Busy?' spat Kirsten, running out of breath as she reached her car. She slid into the driver's seat, started the car, dropped the hand brake with one hand, and then using the same hand, spun the wheel and set off after the Waters's family car.

'What is she busy doing?'

'Gone up to the top level. She'll be briefing ministers and then possibly prime minister. She's indisposed. I wouldn't bother ringing her. Just call me.'

'Don't you take up her calls anyway, if this is the case?'

'Yes, but maybe it's best to keep this one off the radar.'

Kirsten had no idea what Richard was on about, but she agreed, closed the call, and put two hands on the wheel. The rain was still pouring down and she put the wipers on, looking out for the rear lights of the car ahead.

They had a couple of minutes start on her, and she saw the car make a right turn. There was only two ways to go. Coming out of Callanish, there'd be the road back towards Cameron Terrace, the road that would eventually head back towards Stornoway. The other road out to the right headed towards Uig and Reef Beach. If they took that path, it was a dead end, unlike the option for Stornoway, which also meant you could drive to Harris. They made a turn towards Uig and Reef, heading out to roads that, eventually, ended nowhere.

Who knew how long the police would take to get on scene. Kirsten knew she had to overpower the family, bring them in under her watch, keep a low profile, and then allow the service to get them off the island. She arrived at the turnoff towards Uig and stopped the car. She looked up at the road back towards Cameron Terrace and could see nothing. As she looked out to her right, into the distance of a black landscape with only vague shadows indicating hills, Kirsten could see a set of red lights and the occasional beam of light ahead of them. The Waters's car was turning round, edging round lochs and making its way out towards Uig.

Kirsten spun her wheel, put her foot down to allow the car to go as fast as it could, and made her way after them.

Chapter 10

Kirsten found it disconcerting driving along roads with no headlights, but she was keen not to give the car ahead any chance of knowing that she was after them. She wanted to get up close before she would pull up beside them. Indeed, she might even wait until they had stopped. As she sat back in the car seat, she assessed what had happened, and realised that they were now in a much better place than they had been. The girl at least was with her father and her brother. Although they were now tearing around the island, she was at last safe or at least as safe as she could be at the moment with a price on her head.

There were momentary thoughts about the men she had shot back at the Callanish Stones, and she tried to push them aside—thoughts about whether or not the men were still alive. There was enough to do, and she had to concentrate on the road ahead, but where was the end game here? Where could she go? She had contacted Richard and he would no doubt be looking into things, but currently, there was no way out.

She would follow this car down a road that she had to come back on, unless they got a boat off the island, or maybe they'd fly a helicopter in. It would all be very dramatic. The trouble with a helicopter is you could trace it. Nowadays, in the world of transponders, everything could be seen. Even if they weren't switched on, a radar picture would let you know roughly where the helicopter had landed.

Kirsten saw the car ahead coming to a halt as she rounded the bend, and she slowed down, stopping about a hundred yards from them. From what she could see inside the car, there was a bit of commotion, possibly debate about whether they now turned off for Bernera, a small island just off the edge of Lewis with a bridge attached to it, or whether they continued down towards Uig. In her mind, Uig was the better option. At least there were some circular roads there, places you had more than one option to get out from, but she doubted Mr. Waters and his son would be thinking like that. There'd be a sense of relief as well as panic in them, the joy of seeing their daughter, and yet possibly shared terror at what had just happened.

Kirsten hadn't seen any of them get injured, but who was to say. She watched the debate continue, and then the boy got out of the car and walked across the road to look at a signpost.

Kirsten took her opportunity, started the car and drove it quickly up beside the Waters' car, positioning it so close that the driver's door could not open. Having trapped the father, Kirsten stepped out of the car and met Ollie, the older son coming towards her. He swung a fist, but Kirsten casually stepped to one side, grabbed his wrist, and drove him towards his own car. She manhandled him round to the far side towards the open passenger door and shoved him inside before pulling her gun and pointing it at Mr. Waters.

'Remember me? Kirsten Stewart. I'm still with the special services, here to get you out of this. I haven't got time, so sit down, shut up. There'll be people coming after us, so we need to get going from here, okay? Firstly, Innocence is going to get into my car. You, then, Mr. Waters, are going to take this car and drive it about a hundred metres up the road to Bernera. You'll then leave it there. Come back to this car. I will then take over the driving. We're looking at a get-out plan to get you clear of here, because if we don't, the three of you will be dead. You've had a lucky escape, so far. If I hadn't managed to trace you, you probably would all be dead along with those two clowns that kidnapped your daughter, so no chat, just do as I've said.'

'Yes, you were with us at the house but how do I know you're not from Collins?' asked Mr. Waters.

'Apart from saving your life at your own house? Well, I haven't fired the gun. All he wants is you dead, especially your daughter. A non-breathing witness doesn't work in the courts, so shut up, get on with what I've said. Innocence with me.'

Kirsten opened the rear door and pointed her gun inside. Innocence stepped out, and Kirsten took her to the back seat of her own car. She watched Mr. Waters switch his lights on, drive up the Bernera road before parking up, switching everything off, and then running back with his son towards Kirsten's car.

'Ollie, get in the front with me. Mr. Waters in the back.'

'But where are we going?' he asked.

'We're going this way, because if I turn around, we're going to meet somebody coming the other way. We'll possibly head to the beach. Don't worry; it's quite lovely around there.'

Kirsten drove off, leaving her lights switched off, which caused Mr. Walter some consternation.

'You never should have left a safe house. I would have got her. Now I've got three of you to look after.' Kirsten said this in a matter of fact way, but Mr. Waters took it as a scolding.

'That's my daughter. That's my daughter right there. We're family. We don't leave people behind. She's in trouble, we go and help.'

'It's all very laudable,' said Kirsten, 'but at the end of the day, this is too much heat for you to handle.' With that, silence broke out within the car.

Kirsten continued down the road before coming off at a turnoff giving an option for Reef Beach or the road which continued straight ahead to Uig. Kirsten stopped the car for a moment, thinking.

'You said they'd be after us. What are you doing? Why are we waiting here? We need to go somewhere,' said Mr. Waters.

'We need to go to the right place more than anything,' said Kirsten. 'Somewhere we can stay well clear.' Something clicked in her mind as she drove on down the road towards Uig. It weaved in and out along a valley with rocks up on either side. When they cleared it, they came out to a long swinging road, and Kirsten could see the shop and petrol station that serviced this side of the island, but she took a right instead, driving past the community centre and out towards a collection of remotely-located houses named Aird Uig.

Before she could reach the rather difficult road down to there, Kirsten made a right turn off the road, onto a little track that ended in a gate. She jumped out, opened the gate, drove the car through, closed the gate again, and then proceeded uphill in the dark, straining to watch the path that went up there. It took her ten minutes before she arrived at a very small carpark beside a large building. Looking up, she could see a couple of red lights in the sky.

'Where's this?' asked Mr. Waters.

'Forsnaval aerial site. We might be able to force our way in. It's not exactly pretty weather up here and they'll struggle to see the car from the road. I doubt they'll have a chance to look up here. I've also got height so I can use my phone. If need be, there should be a phone inside that building. Everyone out, we're going to take shelter inside because I think this weather's getting worse.'

As she stepped out of the car, Kirsten realised how correct she was. The rain was now pelting down. She hurriedly rounded up her three survivors, marched them up the steep steps that circled round to the building stuck on the side of the hill. There was a metal door with a padlock on it, but Kirsten took a small cutting tool and was able to break the padlock in no time. Opening up the door, she ushered everyone inside before closing the metal door again, and then switching on the lights inside.

'What are you doing?' asked Mr. Waters.

'There's no windows here, they won't see anything on. If you need the toilet, there'll be one here.'

Kirsten could hear the low hum of the electrical equipment that operated the large aerial that sat on the hill above them. She went through a couple of glass doors and looked into a switch room before making her way up some steps, where she found a very small kitchen. Opening a cupboard, she located some coffee, a couple of dirty mugs, and a tap with which she filled a kettle. She switched it on.

'I want all of you to take a drink, sit down, and try and stay calm. We could be on the move soon, so whatever you need to do, do it now.'

With that, Kirsten was the first one into the toilet. When she'd exited, she heard the kettle ping and went through to make herself a cup of coffee. She saw Mr. Waters entering the toilet. A few seconds later, she heard him hurl. *Blimey, the poor guy must be as scared as a man going to the gallows,* thought Kirsten. *He's got a death sentence hanging over his daughter and possibly the rest of his family, and through no fault of their own.*

She tried not to sympathise, to simply just block away any thought of what that family was going through. She had a job to do, and she needed to do it well. Taking her coffee down to the switch room, she found a phone inside and dialled a number for Anna Hunt.

'It's Richard.'

'Hi, Richard,' said Kirsten. 'We're safe at the moment. I'll not stay long. I'll ring you again in twenty minutes. How close are you to having something sorted for us?'

'Well, it could be a while,' he said. 'But yes, ring in twenty minutes, I'll see what I can do. Whereabouts are you?'

'Not on the open line, Richard. You know that. I'll call soon. Have something for me, twenty minutes.'

Kirsten was annoyed because she hadn't got Anna Hunt. With a situation this delicate, she preferred to have her involved. Anna had a reputation for dumping the blame on her troops when something went wrong, and Kirsten fully understood how big a situation she was in. Innocence Waters had seen Kyle Collins kill a man in cold blood. The police force in Inverness have been after Collins for years, unable to pin anything on him, but now they had a star witness, and all they had to do was get her to court. Kirsten mopped the sweat from her brow. She'd been on the go constantly, and she was starting to feel weary from it.

She shook her coat out, the one she'd purchased on the island, and left it to one side to dry a little before she'd have to depart again. Her hair was soaking wet and she was finding her contacts sore. They had probably been in for too long. Carefully, she took out her weapon, looked it over, checked the chamber, put it away again. She may have more shooting to do tonight. She didn't know because at some point, they would have to get from Forsnaval to somewhere else, and who knew who would stand in the way at that point.

Mr. Waters walked in on Kirsten as she was tying her hair up and gave an apologetic look and tried to leave the room.

'It's fine. What do you need?' asked Kirsten.

'I just wanted to say thank you. You were right; if you hadn't been there, we probably would have all been dead, so thank you for the risk you've taken. I'm sorry, I'm just—'

'You're just in the worst situation you've ever imagined, and you have no idea how to deal with it. It's fine, Mr. Waters. Just listen to what I say and do it. Do it quickly and we might all just get out of this alive. Don't go freelancing again.'

Kirsten placed a call back into Anna Hunt, but again, Richard answered. 'She's still tied up, but I've sorted it for you. I've got two people on Lewis, but they're in Stornoway at the moment. Is it easier for you to come to them or me to send them to you? We can do that if you give us your location.'

'No,' said Kirsten. 'We'll come to you. Where are you wanting us to meet?'

'There's a new marina in Stornoway, beside the coastguard station. There, we'll have a boat ready. We'll take the family away by boat. Hide them out.'

Kirsten knew better than to ask where they were going after that, so she simply said, 'Agreed,' and asked for a time.

'Boat's already there,' said Richard. 'Our guy owns it, so it won't be a problem.'

'Fine. We'll get underway now. Should be there in about an hour at the most.'

'Understood,' said Richard. 'I'm keeping Anna updated. She seems pleased with your progress.'

Pleased with my progress? thought Kirsten. *That's not a very Anna comment.*

'Okay. Well, we'll see your man soon.' Kirsten hung up the call, not wanting to be on the line for too long. 'Right, everyone, time to go.' Kirsten assembled the group together before going back out to the car. She checked around the area to make sure it had not been compromised. After everyone was in the car, she drove back down the track to the main road, exiting right after the gate.

'Where are we going?' asked Mr. Waters.

'Freedom. We're heading back to Stornoway. We've got men there who can help you get off the island.'

The man seemed happy. As Kirsten began to drive, Innocence fell asleep in the rear seat. Kirsten watched her brother put an arm around the girl but became aware that a car had begun to follow them. Once she turned a corner where a car couldn't see, she switched their lights on, and the car appeared behind her some few seconds later.

As she came up towards the Reef turn off, Kirsten had a bad feeling. Why was there a car behind her—it was four o'clock in the morning? She indicated and turned off towards Reef with the car following. The roads swung quickly past a small church and then came to a section Kirsten knew well. Take right or left? It was all one loop around the outcrop. Kirsten continued left.

With her speed being held at a moderate pace, she took the left hand turn towards Reef Beach, passing a loch in her left hand side before beginning a climb up. The car behind sped up. Kirsten drove her car quickly up the hill, pursued by the other one. At times, the track was single, narrow, and tight. When they had reached the top, passing a cemetery in the left-hand side, Kirsten took the car down past an array of houses on the side of a hill. As she reached the bottom and turned right, she went past more, all dark and quiet.

She continued to drive round, hotly pursued by the car behind. She spun the car this way and that. As the pace picked up, they cleared the hamlet and were out with grass on either side. Kirsten continued, realising she was close to Reef Beach, and found herself opening up the car for much more acceleration.

The service had given her driving skills, and she was now using them to full effect. When they passed Reef Beach on the left-hand side, she didn't have time to locate one of the whitest beaches and best inlets on the island. Instead, she continued diving around houses and onto a narrow road until it came back on itself, and she found herself passing the church again. The car was up her tail, and as she came out, another car was driving in. Kirsten didn't hesitate but drove straight at the car ahead, causing it to swerve to one side, crashing into a wall.

The car behind her stopped as she took the road back towards Stornoway. In some ways, Kirsten was bemused. They were pursuing her, and yet, they seemed to have just switched off. If it had been two cars, why hadn't one come one way around the Reef and one around the other? Why hadn't they been all over them? It was like they were giving the impression of a chase, without actually doing it. Kirsten pondered this as she started on her way back towards Stornoway.

Chapter 11

The town of Stornoway was especially quiet as Kirsten drove into it at five in the morning. The previous hard rain had changed now to a light drizzle, which could be seen as a mist in front of the streetlights. The sun had yet to pervade and apart from the artificial light, it was dark. Kirsten struggled to see the castle grounds to her right as she drove along Bayhead, making for the harbour. The shops were silent, but on the harbour side, she could see fishing crews readying their boats to go out.

She drove the car along to the new marina further up, closer to the coastguard station. There was a single road out to the car park by the marina and rather than drive straight there, Kirsten parked the car close to the ferry terminal several hundred yards away, advising her passengers to sit there, but leaving Ollie in the driver's seat. Kirsten explained that if anything strange should happen, he should flee as fast as possible.

Kirsten walked a short distance away from the terminal and found herself looking over at the marina from the road opposite. She was struggling to see two cars and Kirsten didn't recognise anything from her department. That could be okay. They might have had to pick up a hire car, but where was the transport for onward passage? Kirsten looked at the marina and saw various boats, but none seemed to have any lights on or be preparing to head out. This was some distance from where the fishing boats were tied up, and she saw cruisers and sailing vessels. As the drizzle continued, she made her way closer to the coastguard station, seeing a building that was all dark, except for a single light up in what must have been the operations room.

The road to the marina went past the coastguard station and was a single road with passing places. If she drove in, she could easily get blocked and struggle to get back out again. It seemed a strange place for a meet. Kirsten stood for a while to see if anyone was about. When she'd gone to find the kidnappers, they were atop the Callanish Stones with a view for miles around. From there, you could get away quite easily in a number of directions, but not here. One road in and one road out, and it made Kirsten edgy.

Again, she stared at the vessels at the marina, but saw no movement. Making her way back to the car, she brought Ollie outside and spoke a few words to him. Then both he and Innocence came to the back of the car where Kirsten opened up the boot. Looking around, Kirsten thought she saw someone in the distance and stared fixedly for a moment before closing the boot again. Carefully, she drove off, making her way up to the car park at the marina, Mr. Waters now sitting in the passenger seat.

'Do you think they'll be safe?'

'I trust my instincts,' said Kirsten. 'They're as safe as they can be. Don't worry. This will all resolve.' Kirsten said it with less conviction than she thought she should have. She saw the man's anxious face but that was only to be expected. There'd been plenty of guns on the go so far and with guns usually came death in some shape or form. It was hard enough for a trained operative like herself to stay calm. Actually, she thought Mr. Waters was doing quite well.

The first streaks of blue were beginning to cut across the sky as Kirsten drove down the single road towards the car park at the marina. She entered and parked the car in the middle of the car park and stepped out.

'Not you, Mr. Waters. Stay there. Be prepared to slide over into this seat if things go wrong.' The man nodded, his face full of fear.

'Are they here?' he asked, agitated.

'Give it time. People don't leap out in these things.'

A car behind them suddenly switched on its lights, flashed them three times before pausing for a few seconds and flashing them twice more.

'They're here,' said Kirsten. 'It could be okay.'

She walked around to the back of the car and tapped the boot twice. When she made her way back to the front of the car, two figures had emerged from the vehicle that had flashed the lights and were making their way across. Kirsten saw two men she'd never seen before in her life, one small and balding and the other tall and blond. They looked mismatched, like they belonged to two different races, but it was clear that the bald one was taking the lead.

'You Stewart?' asked the bald man.

'Code?' asked Kirsten.

'Alpha Charlie Zulu Delta 86954 Alpha Charlie.'

Kirsten nodded. The code checked out, but she thought she knew a lot of the agency staff. Maybe Richard didn't have time to get her someone she could identify.

'What's the plan?' asked Kirsten.

'Boat,' said the tall man and then took a step forward, lifting his hand out towards Mr. Waters.

'And then boat to where?' asked Kirsten.

'Probably down to Oban, then down to Glasgow, maybe even London after that,' said the bald man.

Kirsten looked at the man's hip and could see a bulge where a weapon was. Something in her was not happy. Her hand flexed, readying itself to reach for her weapon. You didn't tell anybody where you were going when they didn't need to know. If they were moving the asset, that was their business, not Kirsten's. And it didn't look like a standard holster on the man's hip either, nor, for that matter, a standard weapon.

'Excellent,' said Mr. Waters. 'We'll be in London then.'

Kirsten looked to her left, realising the man had got out of the car. She was distinctly unhappy about this.

'Where's your daughter and your son?' asked the tall man. Kirsten went to put her hand up, but realised that this would seem bizarre, stopping the man from talking to the agents he was going to go with.

'They're in the boot,' said Mr. Waters. 'Just a precaution. That's what the officer said, just a precaution.'

Kirsten saw the hand fly up from his hip, and the small man was drawing a weapon towards Mr. Waters. Kirsten instantly grabbed her own and managed to get a shot off quickly that hit the man in the hip. Her second shot hit him in the head, and he spun off to the ground. The other taller man was reaching with his gun towards Kirsten. When she managed to get a hand up, he swung round, catching her in the head, knocking her over to the floor. Mr. Waters had reached past her. The taller man engaged with him momentarily before he managed to push the older man to the ground. Within seconds, the tall man was at the boot of the car, throwing it open, gun trained inside.

'Where the bloody hell are they?'

It was the last words he spoke as Kirsten recovered, and shot him from almost point-blank range. Something inside her reeled. She heard a loud scream of, 'No,' from Mr. Waters.

'They're not in there,' said Kirsten. 'I didn't put them in. Get in the car. We need to go.' Waters nodded, and then pointed to Kirsten. At the edge of the car park there were two more men starting to come towards them. Kirsten slammed the boot shut.

'Get in the car, Waters. Get in now.'

A shot rang out, and Kirsten saw the man spin into the car. She ran to him, quickly realising he been shot in the arm, and managed to shove him into the car. From behind his door, she fired over the top with her weapon, forcing the men coming towards her to run for cover. Slamming the passenger door shut, she spun around the back of the car before jumping into the front seat.

The men had now started to run towards her, weapons drawn, but Kirsten floored the car as quick as she could. The men were blocking the exit from the car park, and she rolled down the window before putting her weapon out the front and firing wildly. Both men stood still, firing back, and Kirsten heard a shot ping off the car, but one of her own shots hit a target and the man spun, clutching his leg. The other one stepped across, a barrier between them and single road that would take them back into Stornoway town.

Kirsten grabbed Mr. Waters, pulled his head down below the dashboard and joined him as she heard the sickening thud of the man being hit by the car. She popped her head back up again in time to spin the wheel and get the car heading towards the road back into Stornoway.

'Where are my kids?' the man shouted at her, and she could see his eyes beginning to reel. His arm was covered in blood. Kirsten realised he needed to be at a hospital. As the car drove towards the main road into Stornoway, the single track was suddenly blocked by a car coming the other way. It had put on its beam, blinding Kirsten, but having sounded no horn or even flashed the lights. Kirsten knew it must be someone else trying to block her escape. But they wouldn't, not for a moment.

Without hesitation, Kirsten put the foot to the floor, driving as fast as she could at the oncoming car. She held her nerve, hoping that they wouldn't simply ram her head on. At the last second, the car veered slightly to the side, and Kirsten adjusted her wheel, clipping the car, forcing it into the barrier at the edge. She heard the wing mirror on her passenger side rip off, but her car kept going, bouncing up onto the pavement at one side before Kirsten could steer it back onto the road.

She got back onto the main road, drove down towards the car park she had left Ollie and his sister in. She had told them to hide under a car after pretending to put them into the boot. Something had smacked of being wrong. Too many things weren't done exactly right, and as hard up as Kirsten had been, she had decided to take no chances. They should be under one of the cars in the car park, hidden away. She reached the small roundabout in front of the car park, and took a left in the wrong direction before jumping out of the car and quickly looking under the parked cars that were there. She pulled her pen torch. No one was hiding underneath. She went back and forward quickly, knowing that more pursuers would be following.

'Blast,' thought Kirsten. 'They've done a runner again.' She looked quickly around seeing the Bali House she'd eaten her curry in not that long before. She could see no one along the stretch of south beach and reckoned the young people must have headed off into the town itself. Getting back into the car, she looked at Mr. Waters, and realising he was starting to swoon, Kirsten picked up her phone, dialled 999, and put it on the speaker phone as she started the car again. When the operative answered, she quickly explained the situation.

'Bringing a man into the hospital. His name is Waters. Involved in the case against Collins. That's Kyle Collins. He needs protection. I need officers to go. My authorization is—'

Kirsten battered out a code that was ingrained in her memory. Her eyes darted from her driver's near side mirror to the rear view, looking for any cars that were coming with her. The hospital was only a short distance away, and she asked the call handler to advise the A&E that she was coming in.

'I won't be staying. I've got two people who need protection that I've lost. I am putting this man into A&E. Get officers there to protect him.' Kirsten didn't know how long it would be when she put the phone down before the police would arrive, and she hoped having given her authorization code that they would blue light it all the way.

The hospital was back along the route they'd taken, and Kirsten knew it well from her days of working in the town. As she reached the hospital, she found the car park to be empty. Normally, during the day, it would be rammed, as full as anything with parking spaces hard to come by. She took the road to the left, followed it around, and parked her car in front of the A&E entrance usually reserved for ambulances. Jumping out of the car, she opened the passenger door, grabbed Mr. Waters by the good arm, put it around her neck, and helped him in through the front doors which stood open. 'Kirsten Stewart. You should have had a message from the police.' She shouted this at the top of her voice, for the waiting room was empty. A door to her left opened with a nurse in her scrubs running towards her. 'What's happened to him?' the woman asked.

'Shot in the arm, bleeding badly. I can't stay. I've got two more people to go and find. There will be police officers coming. You need to let them come and stand beside this man when you work on him.'

'We need to get to work on him first,' said the woman, and turned and shouted to her colleague. A trolley was brought out and Kirsten helped them put Mr. Waters onto it before watching them take it through the double doors and into the A&E facility.

Satisfied that Mr. Waters was going to be dealt with, Kirsten made her way back to her car, jumped in and began driving. As she was exiting the hospital, she saw two police cars, blue lights on, come screaming past her. There was a sense of relief because she thought she was leaving the man exposed, but at least now he would have some protection.

As Kirsten drove back into town, she began to wonder where Ollie and Innocence Waters had run to. They had maybe been right. It may have been the best thing to do, but either way Kirsten had lost them again. More worryingly, it seemed she couldn't trust the actions of her own people.

Chapter 12

Kirsten was aware that her clothes had blood on them and pretty soon a lot of people would be asking questions about why there was a couple of dead operatives up at the harbour. She had maybe even been seen from the window of the coastguard station along with a gunshot. Hopefully, they'd been wise enough to keep their heads away from the windows. Regardless, they probably would've phoned through to the police. Kirsten had also used her activation code so that police help would be forthcoming. They'd find Mr. Waters, but would anyone know who the people were that were now dead at the marina?

Kirsten's car had a bullet hole on it and she decided to ditch it, initially preferring to cover the inner ground on the town on foot. She stripped off her wet jacket, allowing the light drizzle to now land upon her t-shirt underneath. Time was precious and she'd need to do a quick scan of Stornoway. It would have maybe been twenty minutes since she'd left in the car. From the marina, say another ten before that. The young people had only a half an hour on her. Where would they go?

She decided to do a quick sprint around the streets, moving quickly but keeping an eye open for any police that were around. She could go to them by all means but any information she gave would be fed back to the relevant authorities. At the moment, her head was spinning. Who could she trust? She had spoken to Richard and he had organised everything, but he was Anna Hunt's second. Had Kirsten been put out on a limb, and if so, why? Would the service want Innocence Waters dead?

Sure, Anna had ordered her to be found. She had brought the family together, allegedly for safekeeping but did the service actually want Collins to get off with the murder he had committed? The service had no particular agenda against Collins. It was the police, who had constantly been trying to deal with the crime organised by the man, who would be delighted to see him inside a cell but to the service, he wasn't anything. They had been called in to help simply to find the girl because of the nature of who the man was. Now it seemed the service was selling her out.

Kirsten turned the corner of a street, saw a police car at the far end, and peeled back to walk round another way. She found herself jumping through hedgerows from one house to another, keeping herself off the street, but she saw no sign of the young people. They could of course, in that time, have made their way down and over to the castle grounds, a large expanse on the edge of Stornoway, with Lews Castle sat dominating the view from the harbour. The castle grounds were a weave of paths and with the new bicycle tracks that have been installed, you could be anywhere up there. Very easy to hide in, the sensible option and one that Kirsten would've picked. She'd been involved in enough police searches in the area to know that even with experienced search personnel, it was difficult to find someone up in those parts. Though, at the end of the day, it was a young man and his younger sister and maybe they wouldn't have been that smart.

Kirsten made her way to the main harbour and could see a number of boats bobbing about at the marina. She stood and scanned them, but saw no movement, only the harbour operative moving back and forward out checking something or other. Had he even been aware of what had gone on in the car park at the marina some half a mile away? Maybe not, the moment was still fresh although the gunshots had echoed through the air.

At a time like this, everything was so fluid. Kirsten had to remind herself that she was again looking for a needle in a haystack but she continued for the next two hours running around the town and avoiding the police. When she stopped, daylight had broken and she took herself to a hotel nearby, checking in under a false ID she carried. She would have to ditch that soon too, but for now, she could tidy her clothes up a bit, get back out and purchase some new ones before she headed off again.

Kirsten took to her room and when she stepped inside, she felt tiredness suddenly overcome her. She'd been up most of the night and while the adrenaline flowed when she shot the two men, there was now a weariness to her. Yes, she wanted to get back out there, wanted to find Innocence, but having scoured the town, she was wondering where to go next. She was used to tracking people, having to find them, but it was usually from their daily lives, not people out on the run, panicked and in a place they didn't know. Kirsten stripped out of her clothes and made her way into the shower, letting the water run over her. She stood thinking.

Who could she trust? That was the key question. Could she trust anyone in the service? Clearly not Richard or had his people been caught? Were there another couple of dead bodies? Guys going about their task who'd been intercepted? No, she didn't like that. She'd have heard about it because they would have called in if they hadn't picked up. If Kirsten hadn't arrived somebody would be on the phone trying to get to her. That didn't make sense.

Maybe this was the agency policy? Was Kirsten getting paranoid? Or was she just thinking that Anna Hunt didn't like her? When Kirsten stopped the sniper shooting at the first minister, Anna Hunt was livid, as she couldn't take the credit. At the end of the day, that's what Anna was about, wasn't it? Maybe Anna was doing this, putting Kirsten out on a limb to get rid of her. Not happy with having her thunder stolen. It seemed extreme, after all, Anna was on her side? Well, somebody certainly wasn't.

She ran her fingers through her hair. She felt her hands shake. She'd killed two people this morning. People who deserved it, but even so, she still felt it. Part of her wanted to pick up a phone and tell someone, talk about it but she couldn't. She would have to remain dark. Kirsten emerged from the shower after twenty minutes, found herself a towel, then stood looking in the mirror. She had to wipe it to take the condensation off it. When she looked, she studied her face. Kirsten saw her own weariness and thought about fighting it but instead, she made her way out and lay on the bed. *Who did it?'* she thought. *Who's compromising me?*

Then Kirsten sat up shaking. She'd made a good call, not putting the young people in the boot. If they had, they would've been dead. After all, the man had got to the boot. He had his gun about to shoot in when he saw nothing, right before Kirsten took him out. At times, the margins were so very fine and yes, she should have been able to keep on top of that, but when it was lives you were talking about, Kirsten, at times, found it hard.

She wanted to switch off, she wanted to take a day and let everything run through her mind but she couldn't. Instead, she grabbed her jeans, put them back on, along with her t-shirt, and made her way back out into Stornoway. She let her hair hang long, but was quick to move into a shop and buy a baseball cap. She also changed her clothing, picking up a black heavy metal t-shirt and a black jacket to go round it.

Where would they go? she thought, as she popped into the supermarket, picking up a croissant and a drink. She also picked up a packet of boiled sweets, shovelling them into her pocket. She needed sugar at the moment, needed to keep going. There was a call on her phone which she'd obviously missed when she was in the shower. It was from Anna Hunt. Kirsten thought about calling back; maybe this was the time to do it, but instead, she put her phone away again. Maybe she'd need to ditch the SIM card. She made her way out from Stornoway across the small bridge that led into the castle grounds.

Climbing up some concrete steps, she followed a short path that led up to Lews Castle and the college beyond. Kirsten stopped at a tree that she would recognise again, for the way in which it bent towards the top. She walked round and round the trunk of it before finding a crack, then she took her SIM card, the special one from the service and she pushed it into the side. Yes, it was time to go incognito but first she'd see what was happening. Carefully, Kirsten made her way into the shrubbery that was off the path beside the tree where she planted the SIM card. She sat herself down for a long stay and watched as people came past, some on their way to work, some students on their way to college.

One after another, she took out the boiled sweets slowly sucking on them, waiting for someone to come to the tree. It took three hours before a man turned up, made his way over to the tree, and started to hunt around it. Kirsten watched as he took out a penknife and started cutting into the tree round about where she had placed the SIM card. Looking around she couldn't see anyone else and deftly began to move out to the shrubbery. The man seemed preoccupied, desperate to retrieve what was inside the tree. He didn't flinch as she got closer. With no one on the path around them, Kirsten reached over, an arm placed around man's neck, pulling it tight.

'You're going to talk; who sent you? Who sent you for this?'

The SIM card would be tracked by headquarters, and they'd have sent someone to find it. The man was saying nothing. Like a good spy, she wouldn't have either. Pulling around the man's throat, she asked him again who sent him. Kirsten was adept in submission holds in her mixed martial arts training. She could throttle someone until they went to sleep, but with her added training in the service, she could throttle them until they didn't ever wake up. Her mind raced over; maybe this was the service coming after her. Maybe Anna wasn't the issue, was it someone else? Had Richard gone rogue? Surely not Richard. He had no signs of it, no markers; more likely it was Anna driving the thing.

Then this may have been an innocent man coming out to merely pick up the intel he'd been asked to do. Whatever was the case, the man wasn't speaking and Kirsten increased the pressure on his neck until he slowly drifted off into unconsciousness. She stopped short of applying enough pressure to kill the man and instead dragged him back out into the shrubbery she had come from. In time he would come to, and tell the agency about the woman who had jumped him. Kirsten would be gone by then, although she was still unsure where. For now, she needed to think and so she continued on into the castle grounds. Who knew? Maybe she would spot them.

Kirsten had not long been in the service, so the number of acquaintances she had was not large. She was under the direct remit of Anna Hunt, and therefore, she found it difficult to believe that this was happening to her without Anna's permission, but the woman hadn't answered any calls recently, it was all Richard. Maybe Kirsten should return the call. Maybe she would get Anna Hunt. She would need to use the special number though, the one Anna had given her that nobody else knew; the trouble was that exposed the phone she was on and the spare SIM card that was her own. Kirsten made her way back into town and bought a pay-as-you-go mobile and then returned to the castle grounds. There, she dialled the number that Anna had given her for any emergencies.

As it rang, she waited to hear who would be on the other end. There was a click as if the thing was transferring and then she heard Richard's voice. Kirsten closed the call before speaking. It was too great a risk, too much to show the man she had this number. It bounced obviously; wherever Anna was, she wasn't contactable. Was she in with the minister? Had she started to travel up and was in a bad area? Kirsten didn't know but reckoned that she could try later. But then again, maybe it was Anna Hunt. After all, Richard was the nice one. Richard was the one who sorted things out. Anna was the one who Kirsten was never quite sure what she was thinking.

Chapter 13

As Kirsten walked through the castle grounds, she knew she had to make a decision about how she was going to act with regards to her own service. *Was there an order from up above to give this girl up, and if so, why?* Kirsten thought that unlikely. *Could someone within the service have connections to Collins?* This was always a remote possibility, but then it begged the question, *Who and at what level?*

Secondly, how far could she trust anyone? One thing she knew she had to do was discover how far this potential collusion reached. Did the police, for instance, have a changed attitude towards her? She was an officer in the service; therefore, they normally would cooperate to a large degree. However, if the service had given her up and flagged her as a bad egg, the police would be on alert and certainly wouldn't have any dealings with her.

As Kirsten knew most of the staff at the Stornoway police station, at least those who had been there over a year ago, she thought this might be the best way to test the water. Besides, she also needed access to a computer and accessing details from a police site would be much preferable than trying to log in via her phone. Anything traced would be to the police station or to a police operative and easily explained away. After all, the police were looking for the girl as well.

Kirsten made her way from the castle grounds towards the police station that was in the centre of Stornoway. As she got closer, she noticed that there were people gathering. There was a number of police, coastguard, and mountain rescue staff and they seemed to be ready to conduct a search on the grounds. Pulling her jacket up around her and baseball cap down over her face, Kirsten turned away from the bridge that would take her across to Stornoway and instead headed out by another route until she was close to one of the supermarkets at the edge of town. From there, she walked back in, making her way to the police station.

Most of the cars seemed to have emptied from the car park and she nonchalantly walked past it several times to work out who was in. Kirsten did think about breaking in via the rear door but she didn't want to give anyone reasons for suspicion against her if they were cooperative, so instead she simply walked in to the front desk and rang the bell. A moment later, the hatch slid back and she recognised the constable she used to work with.

'Hi. What's the problem?' asked the young constable.

'Ellen,' said Kirsten, 'it's good to see you. Any chance we can talk in the back?'

The young constable looked up as Kirsten moved the baseball cap up revealing most of her face.

'Kirsten, they said you were something to do with all that business up by the marina. Nasty work. I take it this is an official visit.'

'I could do with talking to someone, access to a computer and things. If that's okay.'

'Of course, come inside and we'll talk further.'

Kirsten read the girl's face and decided there was nothing to worry about. A buzzer went and she was able to access the inner corridors of the police station. The girl took her into the front room that had a hatch opened to the welcome foyer and sat Kirsten down before going to get her a cup of coffee. When she came back, Ellen sat down with a notebook and pen.

'We're to give you every assistance; that was the line we were given,' said Ellen, 'so what is it you need?'

'Just give me access to a terminal. That's what I need at the moment.'

'Pretty rough out there,' said Ellen. 'They said your guys are going to clean that up, take care of it. We were expecting the murder investigation team over from Inverness. You went to that as well, didn't you?'

Kirsten nodded, 'Yes, he'll be sad to miss this one, Macleod.'

'Yes,' said Ellen, 'Do you remember that time when he first came here? You were run off your feet.'

'And a few times after that, but look, Ellen, I'd love to reminisce, but I've got to get on. Where can I use a terminal?'

'You can use one in here, if you wish.'

'I'd rather be in the depths of the building. Don't want anyone opening that front hatch and seeing me inside.'

'Like that, is it, Kirsten. Okay, come with me,' and she led Kirsten through the corridors, up to a room on the first floor. 'We usually get to do some work in here, away from everyone else. It's a spare one, so feel free. I'll log in the computer for you. If you don't mind, just show me the card and that.'

Kirsten nodded. She expected the girl would have asked her back in the front office, but she guessed that she hadn't used any equipment at that point. It wasn't as if she needed identifying to the girl. Ellen had known Kirsten for at least a year.

Kirsten pulled out her service card and looked at Ellen, who made a note of some details on it and then activated the computer before leaving Kirsten with a screen that merely stated Police Scotland on it. She double-clicked on the internet access button and sat down, thinking what she should be looking up. She typed in Facebook and searched up Ollie Waters. There was the young man that had run away from her, taking his sister with him. Kirsten began scrolling through photographs but was becoming none-the-wiser. He hadn't posted in several days which was understandable.

If indeed the guy had a phone on him, if he was smart and hiding, he would make sure he bought a new one and throw it away every time he used it, and that was the real issue, wasn't it, thought Kirsten. *How smart are these two and where would they go? Why wouldn't they have waited for her? Remember, they'd heard the gunfire and ran, but did they have a plan? That was the thing.*

The father might know in the hospital, but Kirsten would have to go back. As far as she knew, only Ellen was aware that she was in the backroom. Maybe she would tell her superior, but Kirsten would be gone again within the hour. She began looking up Mr. Waters on Facebook and Marion Waters, the mother. Kirsten decided to look on the department's connection and tried to access through the computer but found herself locked out. It wasn't unusual to be locked out from a foreign computer to their own servers, but she had the correct passwords and codes.

Maybe she'd been locked out by someone else. Clearly, the word wasn't out about her, which she found strange. If the service had thought her to be rogue or if the service was operating on a different level, it'd be nothing to lock her out from the police station, advise them she wasn't welcome. The police wouldn't have to arrest her or anything, just simply advise where she stood and to keep her out of their own buildings.

Kirsten started to delve online, searching up anything about the Waters family, but she found nothing of interest. They seemed to be a rather bland family in a lot of ways. Innocence probably had taken the most exciting step in their life by seeing someone killed in after what may have been the last fun instance of their life. Kirsten wanted to talk to the mother, see if she knew where they would go, where they would run, but she was feeling frustrated by having to keep herself in the dark. She tried accessing bank accounts, but without going through the service portal, it was difficult. Instead, Kirsten brought up the OS map of the area around Stornoway, working out where Ollie Waters and his sister could go. If they didn't have a car, walking would be conspicuous. You would get seen as the roads heading out had no pavement. It was fairly obvious if you were on foot. They'd need to take something, something to get them on their way and clear. Could Ollie hire a car? Would he steal one? That was something to ask.

They could have located themselves on the castle grounds, but that was about to be searched with the police taking the lead. If they hadn't have gone there, they'd had to go into someone's house surely. You wouldn't have headed out to the **moorland.** Sure, there would be occasional shielings, small concrete houses used by peat cutters, more in the old days than currently. Or possibly the odd caravan stuck out by a peat bank, but it was a pretty bleak existence. Kirsten was unsure just how aware of the island structures the pair would be. It was doubtful they would go back to somewhere like Callanish, and Kirsten wondered, did they even know whereabouts it was on the island? But did they know anywhere? That was the key question, and one she was not resolving.

Kirsten heard a knock on the door and invited the person to come in. Ellen stepped inside.

'Sorry to bother you, Kirsten, but I had one of your guys on the phone asking if you were here. I said, yes, and I'm getting you to come to the phone, but the line seemed to go dead.'

'Did he give a name?' asked Kirsten.

'Richard, that was what he said. Do you know him?'

Kirsten nodded, clicked the close function on the screen in front of her and waited until she was sure that everything had shut down. She walked over and extended her hand towards Ellen.

'Thanks for your help, but I need to get moving.'

'Do you want me to say where you've gone?'

'No,' said Kirsten, 'and I haven't told you anyway, so don't lie. Just tell them I didn't say.'

'Okay, are you in trouble?' asked Ellen.

'In this job, you can never be sure whether you're in trouble, out of it, or causing it,' said Kirsten.

'If you need somewhere, you can always stop at mine.'

The offer was a delightful one, born out of concern from a former colleague, but Kirsten shook her head. There was no way she would put the girl in the firing line. This was Kirsten's path to walk, and she didn't want to bring anybody else into it unsuspectingly.

'No, I'm fine. I'm better off out on my own. Just say what you know.'

'But I know nothing,' said Ellen.

'Exactly,' said Kirsten. 'Now I need to move. Thanks again for your help,' and she shook the girl's hand. As they walked back down the corridor to the front desk, Kirsten asked if she could leave by the rear exit.

'Of course, you can.' Kirsten departed via the rear door into the car park behind the station and pulled the baseball cap down over her face again. She glanced around to see if anyone was watching. When she couldn't see anyone, she walked round and past the front of the building, clocking two men sitting in a car just up from the entrance. One was reading the newspaper and the other seemed to be scanning his rear-view mirror and both wing mirrors. For a stakeout, they were incredibly unsubtle.

Kirsten kept walking, knowing she would've been tailed had she have come out the front. She made a left into the street, just above the police station. As she walked along, she saw another car, this time with a man and a woman in it. As she walked past it, the two started to embrace and kiss, but without looking to her right, she noticed that the woman's eyes were open and looking out of the car, focusing on her. Kirsten reached the end of the street, turned left, and ran. As soon as she saw a street with rear gardens, she hopped over a fence into one, and started making her way along over each hedgerow. One older man was sitting, pulling a plant, when Kirsten popped up beside him.

'What in blazes are you doing?'

'Sorry, tad lost,' said Kirsten and vaulted over the next fence. She heard the man grumble as she continued on her way, but soon she was down towards the castle grounds. Kirsten lingered by some of the emergency vehicles, and managed to pick up a yellow bib, putting it around her shoulders and marched off into the grounds as if she had a purpose. She continued to walk through the grounds, out the other side, until she got to a small patch of woodland, where she stepped off the path, locating herself behind a couple of trees. She would need to make a phone call quietly, but at least she knew she'd shaken her tail now.

Somebody badly wanted her closed down, unable to complete her task of bringing the girl in. Kirsten wondered who. But one thing she was sure of was that these were not agency people following her around. She felt they were sloppy and she had been trained better than them, so much so that clocking them on the stakeout was obvious. That being said, she was out on her own as was Ollie and his sister. If she was doing her research, other parties would be too.

The research was proving a problem. She was good at this sort of thing, but she didn't have time and she didn't have space to do it. If it was somebody inside the organisation that was trying to close her down, she might be able to assume that most of its workers were merely following orders. If they hadn't locked her out, she might be able to talk to one of them, get some information like she normally would. Who strictly knew about her mission? Not many. Kirsten picked up her mobile phone, dialling a number for someone she knew within the service. Richard had always said that Anna never really trusted Justin Chivers, the section's computer geek. The man could find anything, having great expertise in trolling through records, collecting data from here, there, and everywhere. He was perfect for what she needed. Even if he was a slime ball, it was time to talk to Justin.

Chapter 14

' Justin Chivers.'

'Hi, Justin. I haven't caught you at a bad time, have I?'

There was a momentary intake of breath, and then what sounded like a little bit of scurrying. Justin gave a cough and Kirsten heard a door shutting. 'You don't normally call my phone, not this one. It's the private number I gave you.'

'And? If you gave me a number, of course, I'm going to call it.'

'I gave you it for, how shall we say,' said Justin, 'romantic liaisons. Somewhere where you could ask me about things outside of work.'

'What makes you think I'm not asking you about that now?'

'You're out on a job somewhere. I can tell this. If I really wanted to, I could probably hack in and find out where you are. I find it a little strange that you're contacting me. Richard said you'd gone dark.'

That was something, thought Kirsten, *Richard said I'd gone dark. The agency wouldn't be expecting me to contact, and yet it's been blocked. Lines to Anna are blocked. If I phoned in, it would be directed to Richard or Anna anyway because of my status. That put a different face on it.*

'I am dark,' said Kirsten, 'and I need your help.'

'You know I should refer you straight to Anna. It's not my place to take stuff like this. You're meant to place it with Anna or Richard, and they filter it to me when you're dark.'

'Where are you at the moment, Justin? I heard a door close.'

'It's my special phone, so I didn't want anyone to hear in case I had to put on my Romeo voice.'

Kirsten found herself shaking her head. If she hadn't been sitting behind a clump of trees, hiding away from the rest of the world, she might have burst out laughing. Justin Chivers was the world's worst Romeo. If anything, he was a lech. Kirsten pitied the poor woman who ever got involved with him, but he wasn't an idiot. If anyone was calling him, he knew how to keep separate private business from work, at least while he was in the office. What he would tell them in the bedroom was entirely another matter.

'Justin, I need you to start looking into the Waters family again.'

'I did that. We've searched them. I've put everything up on Anna's desk. You should have it all.'

'I don't, so you're going to have to run it to me.'

'What do you mean you don't?'

'I had certain details when I started this job, the briefing and that, but I need something deeper.'

'I'm all ears,' said Justin, 'Go on.'

'The girl that saw the killing, Innocence Waters.'

'You mean the one tied in with Collins?'

'Exactly.'

'You're involved in that? I heard there was a couple left dead in Stornoway this morning.'

'Justin, don't talk about it. I need you to do something for

109

me.'

'Okay,' said Justin, 'but you know I'll have to flag it up. I'm happy enough to get you this stuff, but you know I have to put it up the line. You're dark, and you're coming to me for information. That's fine, but I have to flag it.'

'No, Justin. You don't.'

'What do you mean, I don't?'

'I said you don't. You need to keep this between you and me.'

'Kirsten, what's going on?'

'Where are you?'

'In work. Where do you think I am?'

'That's not what I meant,' said Kirsten, 'I mean whereabouts in work are you.'

'Inverness. They pulled us up here when everything went down with Collins. I'm working out of your office.'

'Where's Richard?'

'What is this?' said Justin. 'He's here with me, but what is this?'

'Are you due lunch soon?'

'Well, yes.'

'Maybe you want to go for lunch,' said Kirsten, 'and I'll call you.'

'I can call you. I've got the number here. I take it this is a pay as you go.'

'Yes.'

'Well,' said Justin, 'I'll call you back, hang on to it, and you can dump it after.'

'You know I should dump it now.'

'Hey,' said Justin, 'you're the one coming to me. You're the one saying you can't talk here. I'm open. I'm ready. I'm available.'

'Do you tell all your women that?' Kirsten couldn't help herself. She knew she shouldn't have done it afterwards.

'Hey, there's no need for that. You're asking me to go out here on my limb for you. You may not want to take me into your bedroom, but the least you could do is show me a bit of respect.'

He is right, thought Kirsten, *but he's such a lech it's hard to give him credit when credit's due.*

'Okay, I'll ring you in twenty minutes. Is that enough?'

'Yes, but what are you going to need from me? Should I be taking my laptop with me?'

'I'm going to need you to delve into things, and I want you not to have it on any record.'

'Oh, right,' said Justin, 'I'll take my own then, not the work's.'

'Exactly,' said Kirsten, 'Twenty minutes. I'll call you in exactly twenty minutes.'

'Yes, yes, I know the protocol, but this better not get me into any trouble. You know some of them here are just looking for an excuse to kick me out.'

'You shouldn't put your hands where they're not wanted,' said Kirsten. She then heard him take a deep intake breath. 'Before you say anything, no smutty jokes about me and where your hands are going.'

'As if I would,' said Justin in a completely unconvincing tone. 'Twenty minutes.'

Kirsten hung up the phone. Something was going on. She hadn't declared herself to have gone dark. They knew she was operating and trying to find someone, but she wasn't dark. She didn't have the asset properly, not anymore. She'd called in to deliver, and it was somebody completely different who tried to kill her.

The next twenty minutes were a hell for Kirsten. She had questions to ask, things she wanted Justin to talk about, but she had to wait patiently. She would ring him, make it look as if he was getting an opportune phone call. She really hoped nobody was watching him as he went for his lunch.

Exactly twenty minutes later, Kirsten placed her call. 'Hi, mum,' said Justin.

'I hope that's not the way you really see me,' said Kirsten, 'but don't say anything else. I'm looking for anything around the brother, Ollie Waters. He's got a Facebook page. I want to know where else he is online. I need you to dig out anything connected to the Isle of Lewis, possibly the Isle of Harris as well. In fact, expand out to the Hebrides, anywhere he can get to from Stornoway.'

'I take it you mean the car's running well. That's how you would get there to get your flowers, isn't it?'

Kirsten reckoned Justin must be being watched. He was starting to talk like he was communicating with his mother. Maybe answering the questions could be a bit difficult.

'I'll just take a look for you, mom. You really should learn to do this surfing yourself. You're lucky I'm in a cafe at the moment, and I've got my laptop with me. Yes, of course, I can use the phone, but you know how things are.'

Kirsten sat and listened to Justin rabbiting on as if he was speaking to his mother. There was talk about the dog, what had happened to it. The lady across the road who had got run over the week before, and then the pensions were going down again. For fifteen minutes, he rambled on the phone without Kirsten saying a word. After the conversation took a spin into politics, and then back to general reasons for hospitalisation, Justin said something that made Kirsten suddenly hone in,

'Forty-five miles to the west?'

'Is that a place?'

'That's the thing about staying in these places, the sort of place you would go to if you wanted to get away from it all, mum. It certainly is. It's like when you go down to the toy store if that was your starting point, you'd take the road out to the southwest. Oh, it's well down. Well down. Well down past that fishing place, and then on out. A right after the terrace housing, you keep going down, then before you get to that load of rocks, you take the left and it's the island on the right. The bridge? Yes, definitely the bridge.'

Kirsten thought, *Starting point, Stornoway and the roundabout at the toy store. Southwest road out, the terrace, Cameron Terrace, where she'd been. Towards the rocks, the Callanish Stones, take the left. You would drive out towards Uig taking a right onto Bernera, and it had a bridge.*

'Whereabouts.'

'Wendy's. That's where it was. Wendy's.'

Kirsten thought quickly. *Wendy's, he must mean to the west over the bridge, where then?* 'How far west?'

'250? It never cost that much.'

250 metres to the west, thought Kirsten. 'Then?' she asked.

'Nellie was there too, wasn't she? What age is she now? Maybe two?'

'North, two miles. Would it be two miles? Is that the spot?'

'That's where I would go, mum, if I was you. It's certainly a great-looking place.'

'How many people are watching you?' asked Kirsten.

'I'm not sure when they went, the Joneses, but I'm thinking it was possibly three years ago. It seems a nice place.'

Three people watching him. 'You're a star, Justin. Why are they

113

there?'

'It was their cousins that first recommended it. I'd always go and stay with a cousin if I could.'

Kirsten got the message loud and clear, it was a place owned by Ollie and Innocence's cousin. 'Are they the same name?'

'Yes, that's what I said, the Joneses.' Kirsten memorised the location detail. She needed to get a car, take it out towards Bernera. From what Justin was saying, he must've discovered a cousin called Jones out in Bernera, 250 metres west of the bridge, approximately two miles north.

'I guess I better scrap this phone. I might need you again. Have a good lunch.'

'Okay, mum.'

'Thanks for that.'

'You know anytime, I'd do anything for you.'

Kirsten didn't miss that one either. It wouldn't be Justin if he wasn't holding out his arm for a woman. She shook her head, closed down the call, and took the sim card out of the back of the mobile. Carefully, she snapped it and then threw it into the undergrowth. She took another sim card out of her pocket and placed it in. It was fresh and ready to go. Looking inside her jacket pocket, she picked out an ID and noted the driving license that came with it. She'd either have to walk up to the airport or down to the ferry terminal to pick up a car, which wasn't ideal.

Then she thought of the other hire company, the one that did the pickup trucks. Maybe that's what she wanted. She'd certainly be much more in disguise driving around in a pickup truck, especially from the hire company. They were everywhere up and down the island.

With that, Kirsten picked herself up and walked into town.

Twenty minutes later, she was sitting in the front of a hire car. It turned out that they had no rucks but there was a car available. As she took the road out of Stornoway that she'd only come back on that morning, she felt tired again, but now at least she had somewhere to go. She would try and rest as she drove. Not always easy to do, but she needed to get on the move.

She'd have to trust Justin. He would have analysed the pictures in front of him, seen the Facebook postings of Ollie and Innocence. He would have assessed the data, and that was why he was sending her where he was. The man had spent fifteen minutes on it. To Justin Chivers, that was the same as a three-hour search made by Kirsten. As she continued to drive and take the undulating road that made its way across the moor towards Cameron Terrace, Kirsten thought hard about what was going on back at headquarters. Somebody had said she'd gone dark. The only authorisation for that could come from Anna, but Anna had called her earlier in the day. Kirsten did not like where her mind was going with this.

Someone in the office was playing. Someone in the office was surely connected to Collins. It could have been Anna; after all, she called her, which no one else would do if they've been told she'd gone dark, but then Justin had been the one organising everything. She hadn't heard about any more bodies being found, any of her agents being disposed of, the ones who would have met her. If Richard had been genuine, they'd have come. Or had he told Anna, and she'd intercepted him, and instead sent her cronies instead.

Kirsten would have to remain dark and find Ollie and his sister on her own. Once she had them, she could keep them safe until she sorted out what was truly happening.

Chapter 15

Kirsten continued in her hire car away from Stornoway that night, eager to check out the details given by Justin on the holiday home in Bernera. She had heard nothing else about Ollie and Innocence, and nothing had come through in the news. No news was probably good news, meaning they were still hiding out, so far not found, but Kirsten reckoned it wouldn't stay like that for long. The sort of people after them had their ways and means of finding people.

The night was dark when Kirsten crossed the small bridge onto Bernera, a small island off of Lewis. Then, she followed the road round making her way along the island before cutting back on herself. As she was rumbling along, Kirsten saw car headlights behind her, and so decided not to head straight for the holiday home, but instead see if the car was following her.

She turned this way and that, one eye ever on the rear-view mirror. The good thing about a place like this was that most roads were single-track with only passing places, and it's unlikely you would be going to many of the destinations unless you lived there. The far end of Bernera was Bosta Beach which had an iron age settlement, and was a spot for tourists to camp at. For this reason, the main road through the island was probably the busiest but this time of year, there weren't that many people going there.

Kirsten turned down one road and parked up at a house by the shoreside, which was in darkness. She looked out into the choppy water, the wind now rising, and marvelled how it was never quite black despite the darkness, but a collage of deep blues and even a touch of silver despite the moonless night. Coming out from her car, she sauntered her way to the front door of the house, removing a pick and opening it with ease. Not everyone was an expert in getting through locked doors, but Kirsten had been at the front of the queue for training on it. As long as it was a relatively modern door, she had no problem getting inside. This particular door was not very well locked, and she could see no alarms on the house. Kirsten was not worried even if someone was in because she was only using the house as a decoy.

As she made her way through the dark house into the sitting room, she looked out of the window and saw the car that had been following her pull up outside the drive. A man got out, difficult to see in the light, but certainly with a muscular build that wasn't female. Kirsten watched him come to the front door, but by that time, she had moved to the rear of the house, exiting out the back. She made her way around to the front and began looking in the window and saw the man sneaking about inside.

She went over to his car, checked the number plate, clocked it into her memory, and then got inside her own car, switching it on and driving off. As she rounded the hill from where she'd come down to the house, she saw the man running out of it, and starting up his car again. Kirsten continued around the island staying away from the holiday home she was intending to go to, instead making her way down to a small pier at the eastern side of the island. On arrival at the pier, she could see the large green building that housed many of the incoming fish stock and other paraphernalia around this particular harbour, but everything was on a small scale compared to Stornoway.

When she left her car, she was able to quickly run the length of the building and stand in behind it before another car pulled up in the car park. Peering out, she watched again and saw the man coming towards the building, but he stopped before entering. Instead, he shuffled his way down towards her. Kirsten stood to one side, and as the man came past, she cracked him on top of the head, causing him to fall to the ground. He sat moaning. Before he could arise, Kirsten got back into her own car and drove off.

She thought about going directly to the holiday home, but if there was one car here, there was always the possibility there was another, and so she continued her tour of the small island, and this time turning into a rather morose-looking house whose curtains were open, yet windows were dark. It seemed there was no one at home.

Kirsten parked her car at the rear of the house, so no one from the road could see. Making her way around to the front door, she went to take out her lock-picking gear again but found with a touch that the door swung open. She was well aware of island hospitality and the fact that many didn't lock their doors, but they didn't leave them swinging open like this in the wind either. Kirsten's heart began to thump. Somebody must be inside. Someone was up to something, and she was about to find out who and what. She crept in carefully, aware they probably would have seen her park the car from behind. Yet she was trying to be as nonchalant as possible, make out she hadn't realised anything so far.

Kirsten made her way up the stairs and stepped onto a small landing looking across at two bedrooms. There was a door just off to her right, and as she approached it, she saw a hand move from beyond it, coming around towards her face. Instantly, Kirsten moved to one side, stepped forward, and grabbed the waist of someone, before pushing them back into the frame of the door. The person cried out, but Kirsten didn't stop, driving a knee up into their stomach. They bent over and she slapped her hand across their mouth, holding their hair, and driving them down to the floor onto their knees.

'Do you not believe in electricity in this house?' said Kirsten and delivered a kick to the stomach of what appeared to be a man who was not overly well-built. When Kirsten lifted him up, she found he seemed strong of will, for he refused to say anything back to her.

'Now, that's a bit cheeky, isn't it? You come all this way, you try to jump me, and now you won't even talk to me about who you are. What's going on?'

Kirsten then held the man up by his neck, pushing him up against the doorframe and staring into eyes that were not afraid. Well, at least not of her.

'Tell me what's going on. Why are you here? It's an empty house.'

The man shook his head, and Kirsten held him tight, wondering what exactly was going on. If she'd been followed to Bernera, what did that mean? Kirsten took a moment to steady herself. A man had come around with her, so clearly, they'd been tailing her onto this part of the island. Had they got more people to come in and start searching everywhere? If this was a house that Innocence and Ollie were using as a hide-out, it's unlikely they would have put the lights on. Maybe these men were checking all the houses that seemed abandoned, those for whom the owner was not in. Kirsten's plans had just changed. She needed to find them quickly because who knew how many people were out here searching.

'How many people have you got on the go? Tell me,' said Kirsten, but again, the man said nothing. She held him tight by the throat. 'I told you to tell me, and enough of that.'

The man shook his head, so Kirsten slammed him hard, causing his head to knock off the door frame. She let the man fall to the ground. She held him with her foot, and tied him up with rope, his hands behind his back. Then she shoved cloth in his mouth and tied that tight, too. Next, she took the man outside to her car, opened the boot, and threw him in. She needed to know who he was, why he was doing this, but she was also buying herself some collateral. There's always a chance that somebody might want the man, and you can maybe do a deal.

Back in her car, Kirsten drove off, this time heading towards the holiday home Justin Chivers had indicated. On her way, she saw a car coming towards her and watched in the rear-view mirror as it spun around and followed her less than thirty seconds later. Once again, Kirsten went off on her detour, eventually losing the driver of the other car. She sped off round the single-track roads, and coming close to the holiday home again, Kirsten parked up a quarter of a mile away. She drove the car through a gate at a field behind a wall. In daylight, the car would be seen easily, but not at this time of night.

Thankfully, there was no rain as Kirsten made her way along to the house. She found herself having to negotiate several walls before she saw the holiday home in the distance, a simple cottage affair, almost completely dark. Despite this, Kirsten did the last three hundred yards flat on her belly across treacherous ground.

As she got close, she ran up, putting her back alongside a wall, and shimmied around towards the front door. The front door was awkward. Kirsten stared through its glass panels and saw a chime on the other side, which would be counterproductive to a stealthy approach. She sneaked off again, making her way around the outside of the building, arriving at the rear door. The lock for it was a basic key and Kirsten had it picked inside of twenty seconds. Slowly, she pushed the door open, watching carefully in case there was a chime on the other side similar to the front door. The rear door was of solid wood and no such pre-empting was possible.

Kirsten stood at the back door listening to the sounds of the house, and then she closed it gently behind her. She heard snoring. Kirsten looked ahead of her and saw a small kitchen with a door at the far end. Cautiously, she tip-toed across before appearing out into the small hallway beyond. There appeared to be two rooms off it. Kirsten reckoned one must be a living room, the other a bedroom. There must be other rooms off the corridor because there was so far no toilet and no bath.

Kirsten crept forward and thought she heard more snoring in the distance. Carefully, she made her way along in the main corridor and thought she could hear somebody in a far room. Kirsten reached the door and peered inside. On one side of a double bed was a man still dressed and snoring, his chest rising up and down in the dark. Beside him was a girl, much smaller.

Kirsten reckoned she'd found them, but she heard a sound

behind her and stepped away, keeping herself in the dark. Slowly, two feet made their way along the corridor. Kirsten saw the gun at the front end of a hand. She waited, letting the person get closer. She had to time it right, but if she did it, she might be able to keep everyone where they were for the next three or four hours.

Kirsten edged forward, then waited for the foot to move again. She saw the gun protruding ahead, reached forward with her hand, and she instantly shoved the hand against the far wall while the gun dropped from it. Her other arm went up above the shoulder of the person, and her left hand was clamped over the person's mouth. She wrapped her arms around the neck, and almost instantaneously, the man began to break down. His strength weakened the longer Kirsten held, and slowly he went to his knees until eventually, he passed out.

Kirsten was waiting for this, but rather than disturb the two young people, she dragged the man into the kitchen and looked around for something to tie him up with. Once she had acquired some rope and was happy that the knots were secure, she tied a cloth into the man's mouth as well, nice and tight. Then, she decided to wait, taking a seat in the kitchen beside the breakfast bar. She found something to eat, and slowly tucked into it, waiting for the man to wake up or for herself to be discovered. Everything had just been a little bit hectic so far. As the sun came up, Kirsten reminded herself to take it easy.

Chapter 16

Kirsten sat in the corner of the kitchen, all the lights of the house out, thinking through what had happened. She had a man in her boot who had been tailing her, probably aware she was looking for the young pair. Whoever he worked for clearly was having difficulty finding him. There was another figure in here, one who followed her or had been here, and Kirsten wasn't sure if they worked for the same people. As she was in the house where Ollie and his sister were, she hadn't the time to do any questioning of the man now lying at her feet bound and gagged, and also currently unconscious after Kirsten had given him a sleeping hold that had reduced him to a murmuring baby.

She still had the question of who it was at base who had betrayed them, and at the moment, her gut feeling was a toss-up between two of them. Richard seemed such an unlikely candidate. Everything he'd done in the service was so by the book, unlike Anna Hunt. She was well known for going out on the limb, for wanting to advance. Maybe she was advancing in another field. Maybe the money was better. Maybe there were deals being done with people of influence. Either way, Kirsten was caught in the middle, but her remit was to go and find the girl, keep her safe, so that's the first thing she would do, and for the last hour and a half she'd done that, sitting in the quiet kitchen waiting to see if anybody else would stumble across it.

It all seemed very crass for Anna, as too much could go wrong. Kirsten wasn't sure, but when she thought about the other alternative, it seemed even less likely. Richard was always jovial, a good stick, someone who understood what the field was like, and liked to help out if you were stuck in it.

Kirsten desperately wanted the younger people to wake up, but knew they must be exhausted. She would like to boil the kettle, but she didn't want the sound to wake them up prematurely. She had scavenged around looking for food, but, apart from her earlier feastings, there were only tins as befitting a holiday home and a few bags of tea. One of the tins was tomato soup and another, minestrone. Kirsten was thinking that she could boil these up once the younger people were awake. Of course, she'd have to convince them to come with her again. The last time, she'd left them, gone off with their father, and now he wasn't coming back. Kirsten knew she'd have to move soon, but she was weary of trying to cross the bridge in darkness lest she got blocked. It was harder in daylight to stop anyone travelling about.

If she could get close to another car, they'd have to keep following her. Either that, or it would turn it into a dangerous shootout, something she wouldn't look forward to, but also something she reckoned would be unlikely. Everything thus far had been done in the dark. Everything in secret. The trick was she had to arrive somewhere where her pursuers weren't accustomed to all their precautions and where they wouldn't like doing public executions.

Kirsten heard the stereo in the far bedroom, and then there was a muttering as footsteps ran on the wooden floors. The kitchen door opened. Ollie Waters walked in. He gazed this way and that in the darkness before switching on the light. He was shocked to see Kirsten sitting there with a gun pointing at him, and a man tied up on the floor.

'Don't say a word,' said Kirsten. 'Don't move. Don't get edgy.'

Ollie Waters did not appear to be the calm type. 'What the hell are you on? No,' he said and bolted from the room.

Kirsten swore, then ran after him into the bedroom where his sister had just woken.

'I'm here with the service to look after you. You know that. It's me. You were in the car with me, you and your father.'

'And where is he?' said Ollie. 'He got shot. I heard the gunshot.'

'He got shot?' said the girl, looking distraught.

'No, he didn't . . . well, actually he did,' said Kirsten, 'But he's okay. He's in hospital. It was a good thing I didn't take you. They were looking for you. They were going to kill you there.'

'But that was your rendezvous. That was your people. Why should I come with you? I was doing all right protecting her, my sister, I was. Just go and leave us.'

'Can't do that,' said Kirsten. 'I'm going to take you in. I need to get you away, to somewhere safe.'

'You tried that,' said Ollie. 'That nearly cost us my father. You're not going to do that to my sister.'

'Where are we going?' said the younger girl.

'Nowhere. She was just leaving.'

'I need you now,' said Kirsten. 'Let's go.'

'No. We'll stay here. You leave and take that person in the kitchen with you.'

'That person in the kitchen was coming to kill you,' said Kirsten. 'Good job I was here,' although she wasn't too sure whether she had led the person to them.

'We didn't have any problems 'til you, so just leave us alone.' The boy grabbed his sister and started to walk out the door. Kirsten stepped forward and he swung a punch at her, one which she did well to dodge. As he went with another, she reached up, grabbed him, and restrained him by putting his arm up behind his back before forcing him down to his knees. 'No, we are not going to remain here. We're going into the station, the police station.'

'How do you know you can trust them? You couldn't even trust your own people,' said Ollie.

'You have a point there, but that's why we're going to the police station.' Kirsten knew the people in there and she could trust them. How would she play it from there? She didn't know, but at least in the police station, she'd have a fighting chance. Some people would probably be on her side.

'Maybe we should go with her,' said Innocence.

'Get your hands off me,' said the boy and Kirsten released him, shoving him forward slightly.

'Look, Ollie, I know that you want to look after your sister, but you're not capable of it. You need someone like me. I'm going to get you two to ground and fast. The sun's going to be coming up soon and they'll find my car, and then they'll come here. I want to get you to that car first. Get on the move, get into the police station. I know they're trustworthy. I worked with most of them.'

'You work with the people you called before.'

'Only recently,' said Kirsten. She had thought she could trust them as well. 'Why don't we take a walk into the kitchen,' said Kirsten.

'Did you bring anything to eat?' said Innocence, 'It'd be good if you brought something to eat. I haven't eaten anything in so long.'

'No,' said Kirsten. 'Have we got anything here?' and she pulled the girl's brother with her into the kitchen. 'I know there's some soup,' said Kirsten. 'You can feel free to make that if you want, Innocence. I'm not letting your brother away from me until I know he's going to be okay. He's very jumpy.'

Kirsten watched the girl find a saucepan, take one of the cans, open it, and start heating up some soup. Ollie was being held beside Kirsten and she could see how he watched his sister, making sure everything she did was safe. Innocence found three mugs and poured tomato soup into all three of them and gave Kirsten hers before helping her brother to feed himself.

'If I let you go,' said Kirsten, 'I have to know you're going to follow me. I have to know you're going to stay close and take instruction. If you run off on your own, Ollie, you're going to die and your sister will die, too. You need to trust me on this because things have got very complicated.'

'In what way?' asked Ollie. 'All I know is you couldn't keep us safe.'

'No, I think there's somebody within my organisation who's betraying us. Someone who's setting up these snatches, so until I can work out who, I need to keep you close by.'

'Why do you think somebody in your organisation wants to get to me?' asked Innocence. Kirsten was impressed because the girl's hand didn't shake when she made the comment.

'For what you've seen. The man who did it will be paying big money to people. Police officers, secret agents, we all get bribes one time or another. We do know the boundaries, but most of us have to play the line sometime. We know which side we're on. I haven't been able to work out who exactly it is. I have my suspicions on a few, but until I do know, I'll be standing by your side, keeping you safe. The people we're playing with, they don't play friendly. There'll be one shot and you're dead. As much as I like your enthusiasm, Ollie, just stick with me. Don't go off the handle.'

Kirsten bent down and undid the young man's hands, allowing him to take his soup freely and drink from it. He seemed much calmer now, much more reasonable. Maybe that was just the eve of the storm. Maybe he'd run off again like he'd done with his sister before. Kirsten checked on the man who was on the floor, and then tied him to one of the kitchen appliances.

'Who's he?' asked Innocence.

'He won't talk, whoever he is,' said Kirsten. 'They don't do that, this lot.'

'But surely he's from the man who I saw kill.'

The voices stopped. It seemed Innocence had been replaying in her mind what she'd seen. It was one thing for it to stay fresh with her. Rather useful, too, for police, but if it stayed too fresh, it will continue to haunt her time and time again until the poor girl would be demented.

'Try not to worry,' said Kirsten. 'Try not to think about it. When we get you to the right place, you'll have plenty to think about then, plenty to deal with. For now, just try and keep chilled. I'll get you out of here,' Kirsten told the brother and sister as they drunk their soup before going to wash up.

'Just leave it,' said Kirsten. 'You're not coming back. It'll be daylight in half an hour or so. We need to get moving. It's a fine line I'm walking between them discovering my car and getting on the road again so we can cross the bridge.'

'How'd you find me?' asked Ollie.

'Social media. It's always the same. People give away so much detail by being on it. We have people that are experts in tracking that. Personally, I was able to get to our expert before anybody else.' Kirsten made her way back to the car with the two young people in tow. She kept them crouched down low as they went past the hedge. When they reached the car, she had them sitting in the back, but bending down.

'I'd put you in the boot, but unfortunately, it's a bit dangerous if somebody rams me and secondly, I've already got someone in there. We best drop him off somewhere.'

Kirsten drove and arrived at the nearest village where she saw a post office sign.

Opening the boot quickly, Kirsten hauled the man out, and threw him down. Realising he was just coming round, she clocked him one again on the chin and watched as he slumped over.

Running back inside the car, Kirsten drove off, asking the pair of young people in the rear to keep their heads down. She made a direct passage for the bridge because the sun was just coming up, but as she got closer, she pulled over to one side waiting for someone else to come.

Soon enough, a woman came along in a car and Kirsten reckoned she didn't look like she was trying to spot anyone and so drove off after her. By the time she had reached the bridge, the two were almost in convoy. Kirsten looked around, but she couldn't see anybody looking at the bridge, or maybe they thought because someone had captured her or at least laid a hand on her, that Kirsten was no longer a threat. Had their guard been dropped down? Either way, she didn't care as she drove over the bridge, casting a glance quickly on either side.

Having left Bernera, Kirsten continued to drive back towards Stornoway. It wasn't long before she passed a turn, the long road back up towards Cameron Terrace. The day was beginning and there were some commuters on the road, but she could see another car close by. It didn't take her long to figure out it was tailing her.

She stayed tight to other cars believing that she'd be safe if she had people around her. Despite this, a couple of times, they'd turned off or she'd lost them, and she'd find herself having to drive at pace to keep up with the main group of cars. It wasn't long before they were on the edge of Stornoway and Kirsten drove along Bayhead before cutting up towards the police station located in the back streets of the main town. Rather than drive up to the front door, she drove into the car park with all the police vehicles. As soon as she did so, a couple of officers came running out to see what was going on.

Kirsten stepped out of the car, waving to them, 'Jan, Michael, been a while. I need to bring these two inside.'

She opened the rear door, pulling Innocence and Ollie out. She saw the look on the officers' faces, the surprise, shock, and the sudden realisation, duty was required. One of them stepped across to cover off the entrance of the car park while the other waved at Kirsten, ushering everyone inside.

They were taken through and up to the upstairs room that Kirsten had occupied before when she was alone with a laptop. Here they stood and Kirsten watched the door carefully, keeping the two young people off to one side behind her. The police station was relatively safe ground, but who was to stop someone paying enough money from just walking in and shooting them. But at least she was holed up for now, and she'd get help from CID. She'd get one of their safe houses, keep the young people from danger. Things were starting to look better.

Chapter 17

Kirsten knew most of the officers at Stornoway Police Station, but the CID Lead, Detective Sergeant Andrea Lumley, was a new name, and Kirsten was apprehensive about how the woman might take to her. Everyone else knew Kirsten. She had worked with them personally, some quite closely, but DS Lumley had nothing to go on. The situation she was about to be put in was not going to be a pleasant one.

Ollie and Innocence were kept in a small room at the rear of the station, but Kirsten made sure that beverages and food were brought to them. She sat in DS Lumley's office with a coffee in front of her, as well as two rounds of toast. Kirsten greedily wolfed them down while waiting for the sergeant to arrive and was on the point of asking for another round when a tall, fair-haired woman walked in. She was a lot older than Kirsten, although nowhere near retirement. She took off her jacket, hung it up, and faced Kirsten.

'You must be our illustrious Kirsten Stewart,' said the woman. 'I'd like to say I'm pleased to meet you, but frankly, you're just causing a lot of trouble for me. What is it I can help you with?'

'I'm sorry to be a hassle, but we have a situation currently developing within the department. You probably recognise the two people I brought in. Well, at least one of them. Innocence Waters is a key witness in a potential murder by Kyle Collins. We need to get her safe and somewhere that other people will not be able to get at her. There's been several threats on her life already. I've been tailing her over from Inverness and as you're probably aware, her father was shot recently.'

'Yes. The incident down at the coastguard station, right by the new marina. Still clearing that one up. Talk of a team coming over from Inverness to harass me. Are you going to tell me you were involved in that?'

'Very much so. Please, Sergeant, take a seat. This could take a while.'

Kirsten relayed the details of having brought the Waters family to what she thought was going to be a safe handover, only to find that the people picking her up were out to kill the four of them. Kirsten then relayed the detail of having to search for Ollie and Innocence again. The sergeant nodded when Kirsten spoke of the man tied up in Bernera and almost gave a chuckle.

'Do you think your department's turned against you?'

'I don't know,' said Kirsten. 'There's something not right.'

'And yet you came to this police station?'

'Yes, because one, I knew everyone here. Well, most of you. And I know that you're fairly sound. I thought we at least would get refuge for an hour or so. The two young ones are exhausted. They've been on the run and they're also pretty scared. I need to put them somewhere. I need a safe house because I fear if I stay too long in the station that you could be on the end of this trouble.'

Andrea Lumley's eyes flicked up. She had long eyelashes and Kirsten couldn't see any mascara on them. Her nose was pointed and the flesh of her cheekbones tight, but she wasn't unattractive, rather Roman in her appearance, with blonde hair descending to her shoulders. Kirsten watched her begin to chew as she thought about what Kirsten was asking.

'And what's the plan from there? We get you a safe house and then what? The longer your guests stay with us the more hassle there's going to be. There's already two dead.'

'I'm appreciative of that, and maybe you could do with us off your hands, but Innocence Waters is important. Very important. You can check with your higher echelons if you want, but I think they'll ask for full cooperation. My problem is, I don't know who I can trust, so I want you to contact the service recommending a safe house.'

'What will that do? If they've come for you before, how do you know they won't give you somewhere bogus and then jump on you?'

The woman was sensible, and Kirsten noted she was also tapping her nails on the desk. They weren't long and painted, but rather short and stubby. Andrea Lumley had the appearance of someone who got things done.

'What it will do is it will send it through all the higher echelons. If something goes wrong, I'll have a better idea of who did it.'

'Do you want to elaborate on that for me?' said Andrea. 'Because I could be putting people with you, and I want to be assured of their safety.'

'You don't have to be in with us. I realise what you're doing, but you have no need to protect. I'll look after them. In fact, I'd recommend that it's only me. I wouldn't want any of your people in trouble.'

'Well, I can certainly talk up the line, put the call through for you if you're happy with that, but I still don't see how it's going to benefit you.'

'If it's come down a chain,' said Kirsten, 'that means everyone knows about it, or at least the important people. If it goes wrong from there, things would be fired back at them. Questions asked. They'll also be advised of what's going on. At the moment, I don't know what's being played out back home. I went to a meet and ended up having to kill two people who I don't believe were from our service, so at the moment I think someone within our service is playing on the side. Kyle Collins is worth a lot of money. He wouldn't be too shabby about handing it out to make sure Innocence Waters doesn't go anywhere except six feet into the ground.'

Andrea Lumley continued to tap with her fingers before nodding, standing up and turning to the door.

'You need to give me a moment as I go through the processes, check through a few lines with some superiors, and if that's all right, I'll get you your house.'

'Thank you,' said Kirsten. 'I expect nothing less.'

'Feel free to make a coffee or something. You don't have to worry about the young ones. They're down the end, there's plenty of us between them and the front door.'

'I'm not worried about them,' said Kirsten. 'I can see the hallway here, and if there was a face that went past I didn't know, I'd be up like a shot.'

'Like I said, I'll be a couple of minutes,' and Andrea Lumley left the room. Kirsten wondered if she was doing this correctly, but she failed to see what else she could do, ostracised from her links. She had to make someone else do the approach, make sure the service itself didn't want Innocence dead. She couldn't understand why they would. After all, she'd seen one of the worst villains in a long time from Inverness commit a murder. His ship was sunk with her testimony.

Kirsten had fixed herself a second coffee, all without taking her eyes off the corridor, and returned to her seat when Andrea Lumley walked back through the door. She had a very hacked-off face.

'Oh, you're causing a right one here, aren't you? I spoke to my bosses; they're not very happy. They're keen for me to dump you off as soon as I can. I also had a conversation with someone who I believe is your former boss, about the murders up by the coastguard station. Well, they have given me the go ahead to make contact, and that I did a couple of minutes ago. I've been told that your boss is organising the house.'

'Did they give a name?' asked Kirsten.

'No,' said Andrea, shaking her head. 'They simply said you would know it was your boss.'

That didn't help Kirsten at all. If Richard was playing around, he could easily have intercepted the call and done that.

'You speak to a man, or a woman?' asked Kirsten.

'It was a man, said that your boss was unavailable, busy. Look, I've got my contact,' said Andrea. 'That's for them to call.'

Kirsten nodded and wondered about confiding in Andrea about her concerns regarding Richard and Anna. She hadn't said much, and certainly hadn't named anyone. She also wondered how far she could trust this DS in front of her. That was the problem since coming into this side of the business. You never know who wronged who, who was doing what. There were favours, and back-handers paid here, there, and everywhere. While a lot of them wouldn't have been as outright criminal as this, most of the people you work with were used to making deals.

'Did he say where the safe house was going to be?'

'No, but he'll contact within the hour, and then we'll get on the move. I'll take you up there myself.'

'How are you going to do that?' said Kirsten. 'After all, they're probably watching your car.'

'It's not my first rodeo,' said Andrea. 'Just leave it with me.'

It was over an hour later when Andrea finally came back to speak to Kirsten, advising her the safe house was to be up on the Eye Peninsula, known to the locals as Point.

'Right at the tip, on beyond Portvoller, there's a house up there. Quiet.'

'I do know the area,' said Kirsten. 'Is there any road loop out?'

'Where the house is located is right at the junction, so you can go left or right. That loops back to the main road, but there's only the one main strip of road in and out of Point, you know that.'

'That I can handle,' said Kirsten. 'I just don't want to be stuck down some track that somebody can put three or four cars across. When do we move?'

'I just need to get changed. Then the constable will come and fetch you, and I'll see you in the carpark.'

Kirsten wondered about the strange response but made her way back to visit Innocence and Ollie. As she entered the room, Ollie stood up, fiercely demanding what was going on.

'Sit down. Too much is going on, that's what the matter,' said Kirsten. 'We're going on the move again. Going to get you to the house, and from there we're going to get you out of here, but we may have to lie low for a day.'

'Don't you know where they're shipping us out to?'

'No, it's safer. If something happens to me and you get away, last thing I need to know is beyond what's happening right now.'

Ollie looked bewildered. It was obviously a lot for a young man to take, so Kirsten put an arm onto his shoulder. 'Just stick with it. You've come and you've looked after Innocence, but at the moment I need to take care of the pair of you. There are things going on here you can't understand. Frankly, I'm struggling to understand them as well, but we'll keep going, and I will get you safe.'

Kirsten was disturbed by a knock on the door, and a constable put her head in saying that they were ready for them downstairs. Ollie went to move, but Kirsten moved in front of him telling him to stay right behind her all the way down to the back door of the station. As she made her way along the corridor, she could see old friends looking in, bemused, but giving little smiles, trying to encourage, even though they didn't know what was going on. As they reached the rear of the police station, Kirsten quickly looked out the window, and saw a van there with a plumber's logo on the side. The van door was slid back, and Kirsten pointed to the interior, sending Ollie and Innocence inside. She could see the girl was shaking as she got in.

Kirsten followed her, closed the door, and held the girl's hand in the dark. The door was opened once more, and a head wearing a baseball cap looked inside. The figure had a boiler suit on as well, and Kirsten recognised Andrea Lumley giving her a grin.

'I said I'd drop you off. Now just sit tight until we get out.'

The next twenty minutes were in the dark, travelling along roads and bouncing about in the back of the van. It wasn't the most uncomfortable journey she'd ever had, but Kirsten certainly preferred it when you got a nice seat. The girl's hand was constantly clutching Kirsten's, and she swore she could hear Innocence at times start to pray. Ollie, however, was saying nothing, but his heavy breathing gave away how worried he was.

The van eventually stopped, and Kirsten heard someone get out and walk around. It was probably Andrea Lumley checking the area, making sure no one was waiting for them. After a few moments, the door slid back, and Lumley looked in.

'I think it's clear,' she said. 'I had a good look around. The front door's open if you need to make a run inside.'

'Right, let's go,' said Kirsten, and took Innocence's hands, and moved out into the daylight, struggling to see against the light. She shaded her eyes, made for the front door, opened it, and took the girl straight upstairs and into a back bedroom. Her brother was following, and she told Ollie to wait with her while Kirsten went back downstairs and met Andrea Lumley at the front door.

'Is there any food or that in?' said Kirsten.

'Check the kitchen, there'll be enough to keep you for a few days, if you're that long.'

'Thanks for your help, Sergeant,' said Kirsten.

'Not a problem; just get them off my island as quick as you can. I've got enough of a headache with what's been going on.'

Andrea Lumley smiled, giving Kirsten a nod before disappearing off in the van. Kirsten spent the next two hours by the windows, looking out and watching all that was coming and going, but she saw nothing. In her mind she wondered, was this the safe house? Or was this just another trap from Richard?

Chapter 18

Innocence Waters and her brother had been sleeping, but Kirsten could not afford herself that pleasure. As she walked around the downstairs of the house looking out of each window, there were no lights on in the house. She kept everything as dark as she could, while the siblings huddled together wrapped up in blankets upstairs.

Kirsten hadn't closed any curtains either, wanting to be able to see out the windows to see anyone approaching. As it got towards midnight, she began to watch the road closer. She saw a number of cars go past and was registering them in her head. Some she had noted earlier on in the day heading off into town, but a few weren't familiar. Of those she'd seen before, it would be common to get a few. They may have been out in town all day, but some of them she was seeing several times. It had quieted down after ten p.m. Now after midnight, there were only three cars that came past. However, these were three cars that Kirsten had not seen originate from beyond the house, rather they'd come from the Stornoway area.

They said in the spy game that when the hairs in your neck pricked up, when you felt that something wasn't right, that was the time to listen, time to go with your instincts. So, Kirsten made her way up the stairs, knocked gently on the bedroom door. Opening it, she saw Ollie holding on to his sister as they slept on the bed. Gently, Kirsten woke them, allowing them to come round before sitting them down to talk.

'Listen,' she said, 'I'm not happy. I'm not convinced that we're safe here. We're going to move but we're going to have to do it quietly and we're going to have to go not very far away. I'm going to leave you in charge, Ollie.'

His eyes widened. 'Are you sure that's safe? I mean, who knows we're here?'

'I don't know and that's what's bothering me. I'm hoping only the right people, but I've got a feeling the wrong people do too, so I think we need to move. Grab what stuff you've got. Bring a blanket with you too, Ollie. I'm not sure where I'm going to put you is going to be that warm.'

Kirsten looked out the bedroom window. The night was dark, the moon hidden behind many clouds, but thankfully, it wasn't raining. Kirsten asked the two young people to stay upstairs while she made her way back downstairs and looked at the rear window to plan a route to somewhere. She could see a barn in the distance. This being the Isle of Lewis, it was probably open. She could put the young people there. She also noted that in front of the barn was a car and trusted herself to be able to start it if necessary.

In her head, Kirsten saw an attack coming that night, but probably one person, stealthy while everyone was asleep. It would be quietly done, something that wouldn't upset the neighbours until the morning when they found the remains. If indeed they did. Maybe they were planning to carry Kirsten and the young people away. Maybe they needed evidence for their reward. In any case, she needed to move them as quickly as possible.

Kirsten made her way back up the stairs. With the two young people in tow, she made her way out of the rear door, keeping them down low in the grass. As she reached a hedge, she picked up Innocence and threw her over before climbing through herself. With Ollie behind them, together they walked up to the barn, but Kirsten jumped back when a beam of light came on. She headed back into the shadows, keeping Innocence and Ollie down tight waiting to see if anyone would move, but there was nothing. Maybe the owners were used to this sort of thing with stray cats and other nocturnal animals.

Carefully, she edged her way round and found a side entrance into the barn. She opened it and took Ollie inside along with Innocence. Once she shut the door behind her, she used the pen torch to scan the interior. There were lights, but she told Ollie not to switch them on. She led them to the rear of the barn where a large stack of hay had been built up. Climbing up the stack, Kirsten moved some bales out of the way and set them up as a wall before telling Innocence and Ollie to get behind them. She watched them lie down, and put the blanket over them before moving the bales back.

'Whatever you do, don't come out. I'll come and get you.' Innocence reached up trying to touch Kirsten. She took the girl's hand holding it close to her cheek. 'I'll be back for you. Stay safe; your big brother will look after you.'

Ollie's face didn't give the picture of reassurance; rather he looked quite perturbed about what he was having to do. 'Don't you have a weapon or something?' he asked. 'Something you can lend me just in case I have to defend Innocence?'

'You're more likely to kill someone you know if you don't

handle a weapon correctly than to kill the guys coming for you,' said Kirsten. She didn't really believe that, but neither did she want Ollie having a gun and firing off willy-nilly into the night, letting everyone know where he was.

Kirsten made her way back across the field, again keeping low, and entered the rear of the house. She went upstairs and stood beside a bedroom window looking out at the main road. Taking her weapon out, she checked the silencer, and then waited, wondering if her instincts were correct.

There was barely a sound downstairs, but Kirsten thought she heard the door close, possibly the rear one. She was mightily impressed with how they had come so close to the house with her looking out, and yet she hadn't seen them. For a moment her heart skipped a beat.

Had they been watching all the time? Had they clocked her leaving? No, they wouldn't do that. They wouldn't risk Innocence getting away. They'd have come over and taken them right there and then.

Quietly, she moved to the edge of the bedroom door listening for anyone coming up the stairs. As she pressed her back to the wall, she continued to control her breathing, realising that she was starting to feel the adrenaline kicking in. There was a slight creek on the stairs, and then another one, getting closer. Slowly, she moved along the wall crouching to get a good angle for the door. They probably wouldn't come in slowly; they'd come in quickly, scanning and firing, and she needed to be ready.

Her eyes were adjusted to the dark. She thought they might slap the lights on as well to try and confuse her. Patiently she waited, going over in her head, again and again, what to look for. If a gun was trained on her, she would fire.

The door burst open. She saw a weapon and a pair of hands go away from her, then to the middle of the room, then come towards her. There was a masked person behind it and Kirsten fired almost instinctively. She watched the body fall backwards causing an almighty thump on the ground.

She waited for a moment before stepping forward and firing another shot into the head. Then she raced back to the wall again.

Would there be only one? Would more come?

She kept her mind off the body that was lying on the floor ahead of her, focusing instead on what she could hear. Inside her, something was knocking, telling her she had just killed a man, telling her she should feel something about it; but her training was kicking in, ignoring the moment, looking instead for what was coming next, driving her emotions to the rear. There'd be a price to pay for this at some point, but not now. Now she needed to be alert.

Kirsten stepped up to the door, peered out quickly, and saw no one. She then stepped to the other side of the door before peering back and then looking down the stairs. Again, there was no one. She stepped out gingerly onto the landing looking down. When she did, something caught her eye coming out from the bedroom across the landing. She threw herself to the ground as a shot pummelled into the wall behind her. Kirsten raised her gun and fired once, then twice, and heard somebody spin and fall to the floor. She had no idea if the person was still alive or not, but she had to react quickly because she heard someone moving downstairs.

Reaching the top of the stairs, she saw them at the bottom, and she ducked quickly as they fired before firing back, hitting one square in the temple. Kirsten glided down the stairs into the hall, again, listening and looking around her. She saw nothing until a mirror extended out into the hall.

It was small and often used by people sneaking out of buildings. She'd used them herself, but she knew what was going to come with it, and before anybody could peer out, she fired a shot down the hall as she ran for the door into the living room. She tried to fire a second again but to find that her gun was no longer working. She threw herself into the front room as she heard a shot bounce off the woodwork behind her. Kirsten hid behind a sofa in the room aware that someone was going to be coming in soon. Sure enough, although he was moving stealthily, she could hear him, just the little giveaway steps on the floor.

Kirsten looked under the sofa, and saw the man coming closer. Her gun was useless so she knew she'd have to fight her way out of this one. The element of surprise was gone to a large degree, but maybe she could fool him again. As he came close across the living room floor, her plan was formulating in her head. She needed to hit him hard and hit him fast.

She watched his feet from underneath the sofa step across until they were almost in the middle. The man was less than two feet away clearly scanning around the room looking for her, wondering if she'd disappeared out another door. As he turned sideways to her, she drove herself at the sofa almost lifting it up, careering it into the man's knees. He fell sidewards, taken by surprise, and Kirsten reached up and grabbed the gun hand. A shot went off into the far wall, then another, and she thought to knock the hand down. The gun fell out and as Kirsten reached out for it, the man came over the top of the sofa, jumped on top of her, and throttled her from behind.

She was prone on the floor and he was on top and she was

145

struggling to get him off. Her diminutive size caused her problems at times, especially with much larger opponents. Here on her back being strangled, Kirsten was struggling for any hold to get out of the situation.

Desperately, Kirsten reached out trying to find the gun in the dark on the floor. It was just beyond her reach, but the man on top of her was keeping his grip on her throat and she could feel herself slowly succumbing. The windpipe was being strangled, and she was struggling to breathe, struggling to refuel her muscles with oxygen to be able to fight the man off.

Kirsten thrashed this way and that, but the man wasn't having any of it, and she realised her only chance would be the gun. She was able to drag him forward slowly, but every effort was weakening her. She couldn't reach out and get a hold of his head because he was keeping it perfectly behind her his arms extended on her neck, but she stretched hard, almost touching the gun.

Then the man stretched for the gun, keeping one hand on her throat but reaching over with his other hand, his head now moving from its position clear of Kirsten. She didn't hesitate, reaching up and grabbing his hair, pulling it tight before trying to jab two fingers up in towards his eyes. She caught the corner of one causing him to spin off her, but he was now lying over the gun.

Kirsten drew what reserve she had and flung herself at the man before he could orientate himself. He rolled her over, pushing her shoulders back onto the floor now, throttling from above. She reached inside with both hands, knocking the man's hands from either side and as he fell forward on top of her, she nutted him straight into the face.

She then threw him off to one side before seeing his hand reach for the gun. Kicking it clear, she booted the man's hand three times. Kirsten jumped on the man because he was still in motion, still trying to get up. Strangling his neck, her thoughts then begin to drift. A part of her would have liked to just keep holding on and dispatch the man. After all, he'd been coming to kill her. Instead, once he was knocked out and was off to sleep, she released him. That wasn't her. She'd kill if she had to, but she couldn't take any pleasure in it.

Making sure the man was going to stay down for a while, she searched his pockets before finding the keys to a car that she couldn't see. She also took his gun since her weapon was malfunctioning. Exiting the house from the front door, Kirsten looked around. All the guns had been shot with a silencer, so nobody in any other house seemed to be moving. She ran down the street pressing the open button for the car but found nothing. She turned and ran back the other direction before seeing a car parked further up the street. The orange lights of the indicators came on as she pressed the open button and she jumped inside the black car. She put the keys in the ignition and started it and quickly drove over to the house with the barn holding her protectees inside. Kirsten hauled the straw away and was relieved to see the two young people were still there. She knew they'd be a flight risk, but they'd always have been safer doing that than being back in the house.

'What happened?' asked Innocence.

'Let's just say we have to move house again, and this time, I'm not letting anybody organise it for us. You're going to have to rough it.'

Chapter 19

Kirsten wiped the sweat from her brow as she drove along the Eye Peninsula making her way through the short stretch of land that connected Point to the Isle of Lewis. It was called the Braighe and she'd been over it many times during her stint as a constable in the Stornoway Force, but never as today was she so glad to see it at three a.m. in the morning. On the left-hand side stretched out the sandy edge of the Braighe and she could just about make out the water rolling in on a low tide.

Kirsten drove with her headlights on as she was coming towards town and besides that, all the lights were switched off by the roadside during the nights on this part of the island, a cost-cutting exercise. As she made her way into Stornoway, she thought about the two young people in the backseat, both with their heads down keeping out of the way, who she wanted to store safely while she shook some feathers and tried to work out what was going on. There was nowhere open to buy supplies and Kirsten took the car out on the Barvas Road, a route heading across the moor to the west side of the island.

At certain times of the year, people would go out to the moor to cut peat, leaving the rectangular-shaped black playing cards stacked together. They would dry them by turning them up and making them into little houses before burning them through the winter on their stove. Kirsten had never gone peat cutting but she knew the practice and had seen the people working the banks.

Some people had accommodation near their bank, nowadays usually an old and small caravan. In the old days, they were what was known as shielings. They were concrete houses but now only a few people would stick a caravan out there. There was always the difficulty of getting any services to them.

Driving along the Barvas Road, she spotted one of the caravans in the distance, realised there were no cars around her and killed her lights, taking a turnoff onto the moor. She had to stop and open a gate to get through and drive down the bumpy track and eventually ended up by the caravan. Kirsten told Ollie and Innocence to remain in the car while she checked the caravan, making sure no one was inside before breaking open the door. She ushered them inside and was glad to see there was at least some blankets even if the overall smell was quite mouldy.

Walking around to the front of the caravan, she found the gas, switched it on, and managed to light the fire inside, giving them some heat, but she warned them not to switch on any lights. Of course, that's if the battery would allow, she thought because it may have been a while since the caravan was last used.

Content that the pair of them were now warm and safe, Kirsten drove without her lights on back onto the Barvas Road before making her way back into town. Arriving at the police station, she approached the front desk, getting a smile from the sergeant behind it.

'Are you back again?' said the man. 'They told me you were. How are you doing?'

'Not so well, Jim. Not so well on it. Listen, I need to talk to Andrea Lumley and fast.'

'I think she's gone home,' said Jim. 'Is this all to do with that business up at the marina?'

Kirsten nodded. 'Have you got a phone number for her or address even? I could pop round and see her.'

'Hang on a minute,' said Jim and reached over into a book, opening it to find the number. As he scanned down, Kirsten looked behind him and saw a coffee machine.

'Jim, you don't think you could give us that, could you?'

'What?' said Jim.

'A wee cup of coffee, keep us going at this time of the morning. It's no wonder you guys have it in here.' Jim nodded and turned around making his way across the room for the coffee. Kirsten quickly grabbed the book.

'Do you take sugar?' asked Jim. Kirsten didn't but she said, 'Yes,' to occupy more time.

'Milk?' Kirsten's finger was scanning down the page and then she found Andrea Lumley.

'Yes, plenty of it.' She now was able to see the address, memorising it immediately.

Jim was about to turn around with the cups and Kirsten put the book right back where she had found it. 'There you go,' said Jim, handing her a cup through the window. 'I'll just get that number for you.'

'Thanks, Jim,' said Kirsten and waited patiently while the man wrote down the phone number of Andrea Lumley and handed it to Kirsten.

'I'd give you her address, but you know I can't do that.'

'It's no problem, Jim. You've been very helpful,' and with that Kirsten downed the coffee, commented to Jim about how divorced life must be suiting him, and then handed the cup back before exiting the police station.

After making her way back to the stolen car, Kirsten took it around to the address she had memorised from the book. It was out on the edge of town towards the war memorial that was set high on a hill above Stornoway. Soon, she turned down a street of detached houses, modest, and she suspected owned mainly by people in managerial positions but certainly nothing spectacular.

Reaching the correct house, Kirsten recognised the alarms on the outside. She located the panel in the hallway that could deactivate the alarms and squinted hard to try and recognise the make. She knew she'd have to get Andrea up quick, pull her downstairs and she wasn't sure who else could be in the house. She could knock but she wanted to see if the woman was for real. Somebody had given away where they'd been. Was it Richard? Was it a grass at Stornoway Police Station? Kirsten had her own ideas but at the moment, she wasn't into trusting anybody. She picked the lock on the door, opened it, and heard the alarm start to bleep. Quickly she bounded up the stairs, pushed open the door of the largest bedroom, and saw a man and a woman asleep. She tore across and saw Andrea begin to wake up, her face looking shocked. She grabbed the woman in her nightie, pulling her out of the door, shouting at the husband to shut up and sit down. Kirsten brandished her gun at the same time just for effect and then hauled Andrea all the way down the stairs and told her to kill the alarm placing the gun to her head. The sergeant complied.

'Call your husband down. Anyone else in the house?' asked

Kirsten.

'No, no,' said Andrea quite agitated, and called her husband, Matthew, down.

Kirsten with the point of the gun indicated they both should move into the living room and made sure she closed the curtains while they did so. Kirsten then took a position in front of the pair with the gun trained on them. She still had the safety on because she didn't want any accidents. After all, she was only scaring the information out of the people.

'Who did you speak to again?'

'I told you. When I contacted, they tried to put me through to Anna Hunt. I didn't get her. I got somebody called Richard, but he said Anna was the one running this. He was just relaying information from her.'

'Did you believe him?'

'Why wouldn't I?' said Andrea. 'I had the phone number, I went through the correct processes. That's where I ended up.'

'At any point did you speak to Anna Hunt?' asked Kirsten.

'Not at all. I don't even know who the woman is.'

'What's this all about?' asked Andrea's husband, but Andrea turned, put her hand on his thigh, and told him to be quiet.

'Look, I don't know anything other than what you told me. I've done it. I tried to get you there securely.'

'Who knew the location?' asked Kirsten.

'No one but your guy Richard, obviously because he told me where to go. Otherwise only I knew it.'

'Anybody else in the station?'

'No, but I did get into a van, and then you, so maybe they could have traced it.'

'Have you ever met Richard before? Ever had anything to do with the services?' asked Kirsten.

'No,' said Andrea. 'You came to me. I took a bit of flack off the boys above, and I got the job done. I did what you asked. Why are you pointing that gun at me?'

'In the middle of the night, four men came to take out the Waters girl and her brother. I sniffed it out before it happened. The safe house now has a couple of bodies in it.'

Andrea looked shocked. 'Where are the other two now?'

'You don't get to ask that,' said Kirsten. 'That's on me. Only me. Don't ask that. If you want to be a friend and be helpful, don't ask that.'

Andrea's husband Matthew seemed quite strained. Kirsten thought she could see tears coming to his eyes.

'Just don't do anything to us, okay? Andrea is a good officer. She does things by the book. She's not one of these people that you're talking about.'

'I don't know who I'm talking to at the moment. I've never met her, so pardon me, sir, if I seem a little rough-handed, but I've been attacked several times. Each time I wasn't meant to walk away. If your wife can help me get to the bottom of this, she's going to.'

'And I will,' said Andrea. 'It's not a problem. Just put the gun down and talk about this.' Kirsten put her gun in its holster and allowed Andrea to stand. She went through to the kitchen and Kirsten insisted Matthew follow them making sure nobody reached for a phone.

'Forgive me, it's not that I don't trust you, it's just I don't trust you,' said Kirsten. 'I trust no one. I've got two lives on the line and my own, so I'm playing this very coyly.'

'That I can understand,' said Andrea. 'Look, the way I see it is if you trust us down at the station, and I think you do because you know most of them, and it hasn't been me, it's got to have been that Richard, hasn't it?'

'Why would you say that?' asked Kirsten.

'Well, he's getting all the information, isn't he?'

'But it could be Anna. She might be the one doing it.'

'Then you need to correlate on it, don't you?' said Andrea. 'You need to get contact with her direct, get her to organise the next meet, then you'll see what's what.'

'But if it is her, I might as well give up. We could have the department actually looking to finish them off.'

'Why? When did my department make deals with criminals like Kyle Collins?'

Kirsten took a cup of coffee from Andrea and sat down opposite her on a large stool in the kitchen. She watched Matthew try to drink, but his hands were too unsteady. He spilled his coffee on the kitchen table. Andrea was compassionate to him taking a cloth wiping up and just telling him to sit there because it will all be done very shortly.

'Okay,' said Kirsten. 'I'm going to go soon. I won't be back to the station, it's too risky to you, if you're telling the truth. Too risky to the people there.'

'If all the avenues look dodgy,' said Andrea, 'you can come to me, we'll do what we can. They won't want to be coming to a police station to take people down. Not even your lot surely.'

Kirsten thought about the service. You never put anything past them. If things needed to be done, they did it, regardless of what mess it caused. There was always a way of covering things up, always a way of doing things. There might be a little bloody nose from stuff, but you had to get the job done.

Kirsten left Andrea and Matthew in the kitchen, made her way out to the car, and drove off. She took one of the smaller roads out of town, stopping when she still knew she had a signal and killed all of the lights. With her mobile, she called in with one of her new SIM cards, getting the direct number of Justin Chivers.

'What's the deal?' asked Justin. 'Have you got anywhere with this?'

'Shut up and listen,' said Kirsten. 'I need you to go to Anna.'

'Go to Anna?' said Justin. 'Why?'

'I think Richard's dodgy. I think he's the one doing this, but I can't be sure. I need you to go to Anna direct. Tell her to keep it away from everyone else and organise an extraction for me.'

'Ooh, what? I just barge in and tell her this?'

'Basically,' said Kirsten. 'You do because how else would I get the information to her? Every time we phone, anyone phones, Richard seems to be picking up.'

'That's because Anna's in with the ministers. She's been briefing them on and off for ages.'

'That may be as it is, tell her I need her to meet me. I need to get to her so we can get a proper extraction plan. She can pitch up in Stornoway, wherever. I'll kill this SIM now, but I'll put it back in in four hours' time. You give me the time and the place, and I'll meet her. Are we understood, Justin?'

'Of course, but what if Richard catches me on this one?'

'You keep well clear,' said Kirsten. 'You have to. If he catches you, he may well do something to you. He's out on a limb if we snag him with this, so take care of yourself, Justin. Straight to Anna, nobody else, understood?'

'It might take me longer than four hours if she's in with the ministers. I've got to go through Richard normally.'

'Yes, you do but you're a techie. You know how to work things. You'll get a message to her. I'm counting on you, Justin. You know that, don't you?'

'Just remember, you owe me dinner with this one,' said Justin, 'and that nice red top you used to wear.'

'You'll get dinner but it'll be a McDonald's,' said Kirsten. 'Get Anna for me.' She hung up. Justin was so cheeky. Even at times like this trying to egg a date out of her. Kirsten opened the mobile, pulled the SIM card out and tucked it away. She drove the car back out to Barvas Moor, getting to the caravan about six. Once there, she scoured the surroundings, then went inside and put herself on the front sofa where she started to get into a fitful sleep.

When she awoke she made a short trek out of the caravan, placed a SIM card into the phone, and waited. Thirty seconds later there was a beep on the phone. She checked the text message. Stornoway airport, half-past three.

Chapter 20

Kirsten drove up and down the road at the end of the threshold of the runway of the airport. Anna had said that she was coming on the two o'clock flight, but Kirsten couldn't find a commercial flight that matched that. Instead, she had a flight radar app open, an internet-based tracking system that was able to pick up the individual squawks of aircraft in the air and give you a rough radar picture of what was going.

Now approaching two o'clock there were no commercial flights, but there was a King Air Beechcraft making its way towards the runway. Rather than sit and wait in the car park, Kirsten continued to drive, until saw the aircraft landing on the northerly runway, coming in low over the road and being photographed by a lone photographer.

There was nothing unusual about this. Most visitors to the island found the closeness of the road and the runway quite spectacular, but to the locals, it was a daily occurrence to have a plane flying over the top of your car. Kirsten watched it taxiing in and parking on the lower apron at Stornoway. This was the smaller apron where the commercial traffic didn't go.

Kirsten drove up to the car park beside it and saw a small figure climbing out. It was dressed in black, had a rucksack over its shoulder and made its way out through the gate, straight over to Kirsten's car.

'It's good to see you looking so well,' said Anna Hunt, opening the car door and stepping inside.

'It hasn't exactly been a joy ride.'

'By look well, I mean not dead,' said Anna. 'Now drive, we've got a lot to talk about.'

Kirsten took the car out of the airport and drove off into Stornoway.

'We haven't got long,' said Anna. 'Richard caught Justin talking to me, so I had to make up a tale about him. I'm not sure if Richard bought it, so I think he's following up quite shortly. Now, where have you got them?'

'I'm not telling you where they are,' said Kirsten. 'You've got to look at this from my point of view. I don't know which of you two are dodgy.'

'And you're saying that openly to me?' said Anna. 'I think that tells you who you think really is the traitor in our midst. I take it the girl's unharmed?'

'Shaken up,' said Kirsten, 'bit like her brother, a few scrapes with death, you know what I mean? I had to put quite a few down. I hope they're not from our service.'

'None of them are from our service, because if they were we'd be onto them, whoever was calling these shots. Either that or you'd have been making a glorious mistake. The bodies are all outside people, but they're guns for hire. Nothing I can trace back to anyone specifically, but I'm working on it. Trust me.'

Trust me. There was a word Kirsten heard very often in the

service, a word that didn't mean a lot and yet getting the right answer to that 'trust me' statement was everything.

'We need to get them off-island. Different route, something nobody else knows about except yourself, Anna.'

'You do trust me.'

'No. If it goes wrong with you at the helm, then I know you're dodgy as well. If it doesn't, I know it's Richard.'

'What if it goes wrong with me at the helm. What do you think of your Richard then?'

'Unknown,' said Kirsten. 'I wouldn't have any proof to say that he was dodgy, but I wouldn't have the proof to say he wasn't either. He's too heavily involved in a lot of the decisions made, too heavily involved in what's gone on. I can't ignore that. I had to go round him with Justin Chivers. I don't like doing that, especially with the way Justin is. After all, you always said he'd talk just by looking at a woman.'

'Might be true. It depends if it was a woman who'd asked him not to,' said Anna, smiling.

'Where's the best place to go?' said Kirsten. 'Where's the best place to get off here and keep them hidden?'

'Well, we keep out of Stornoway for a start,' said Anna. 'Better down near one of the fishing villages or even somewhere like Leverburgh right down the bottom of the island. We can get on a boat there, especially an unmarked one. We can make her disappear.'

'Into the system. Richard will have tabs into the system surely.'

'Doesn't work like that, Kirsten. We don't get tabs into the system. All we've got to do is get them there.'

'What's to say there isn't somebody in the system looking out for them as well?'

'Stop,' said Anna. 'You're seeing evil at every turn. You're running wild here. I understand you've been shot at, and they've tried to kill you several times. You're reeling because somebody like Richard you used to trust is doing this to you, so much so you now haven't got a clue if it's me, it's him, or a man from Timbuktu. You need to focus. You made the right call. You've got me up to organise. If it goes wrong with me at the helm, you know it's me. If it doesn't, you've got someone you can trust.'

'I never said I didn't trust you,' said Kirsten. 'I've always just thought you were a bit—' Then she stopped herself, realising this was her boss she was talking to. 'But it's Richard,' said Kirsten. 'That first time, when I had to put the two men down by the camper van back on my first assignment. That was when Richard talked to me. He looked out for me when you didn't.'

'I'm your boss. I'm not your nanny,' said Anna. 'I'd be very wary of people who'd take an interest like that. Your problem is Macleod was too good to you.'

Kirsten scowled at the mention of her former boss's name. 'Don't you say a word about him.'

'Or what?' said Anna. 'Of course, I'll say a word about him. It was his team. It was the place he was over the top and running. You were a little pet favourite of his. I'll admit it, you had the talent and he used it, but you were also his little pet favourite. I don't have favourites. I can't afford to. I can't afford my judgment impaired because I like someone. When Richard came to you and he's giving you all the consoling effort, what were you thinking about that? Oh, makes him a nice man? No, that's not how you judge people in this game. You judge them by what their actions are. Who's done what and when.

You look for the ulterior motive. And sure, that might make me someone who's suspicious of everyone, but I don't have an ulterior motive.'

'Sure, you do,' said Kirsten. 'You just want to climb as high as you can, and you'll use other people to do it.'

Anna put up her hands and smiled. 'Guilty as charged, but it's not an ulterior motive that harms the service. With Richard, you're talking about someone who's harming our interests, all our interests.'

'If it's him.'

'Oh, I know it's him,' said Anna. "Is it only him?" is the question. Does he have somebody higher up protecting— is he running it for them? We're talking about Collins here. He's serious. He's big time in Inverness; he's big time in Glasgow too. He's been on the national register as our main target for ages, and we've never got near him, and now we do, and we knew he had people in his pocket, but not the service. No, you don't do it in the service. If you're one of mine, I'll put you down,' said Anna. 'Without hesitation.'

Kirsten cast a glance. 'You mean, I'll put him down.'

'No, I will. You forget I worked the field too. I didn't get to this position by sitting behind a desk the whole time talking to politicians. I got to this place because I can handle things, I can manage situations and I did them in real-time as well. So, don't come after me like that. If he's dirty, I'll put him down, but only when I know I've got everyone else.'

The mood was sombre as they continued to drive through Stornoway, never stopping anywhere, but instead discussing plans. Anna came up with the idea of taking a boat down to Leverburgh, but she said she'd need a while to do it. She asked Kirsten to stop outside a computer shop, and inside, she found two mobile phones, purchasing them with pay-as-you-go and several other SIMs. Anna made a note of the numbers of Kirsten's, and of her own, and then handed the phones to Kirsten.

'In case we need to contact, you come straight to me on these phones. The only other person you talk to is Justin.'

'You always said Justin blabs.'

'I say a lot about Justin. Some of it's true, some of isn't. Justin blabbering is the biggest fabrication I've ever made.'

'Because everybody thinks he can't be involved and he's kept at arm's length by you. That's a clever one, Anna.'

'It is, but he is a sexist pig, I never made that up.'

Anna waved goodbye and advised that she would contact the father to let him know that the daughter and son were safe. She'd also pick up the loose ends with Stornoway Police, make sure that the murder squad didn't get too heavily involved. Kirsten stopped off and dropped the car before picking up another hire car for herself. She drove it out along the Barvas Moor, making sure no one else was on the road before she cut down towards the caravan. There was nowhere to place the car out of sight, but she did the best she could with it before entering the caravan and telling the two inside to get ready.

'This should be it, Innocence,' she said. 'Ollie, we're nearly there. We're going to take you down to Leverburgh and we're going to get on a boat down there. From there, you'll be put into the Witness Protection Program, far from my department, far from any department except those that need you. But it's my job to get you safely down to that boat, so get your things together and get in the car, and we can get going now.'

'When's the boat coming?' asked Ollie.

'I don't know,' said Kirsten. 'But I'm not going to wait until then.'

That afternoon, Kirsten took the road down towards Tarbert on the Isle of Harris and continued south towards Leverburgh. They passed the beach of Luskentyre, beautiful white sand that attracted many a tourist, but here at the back end of summer, there were fewer about. Kirsten cut away from Leverburgh, routing into the side roads on the east of the island of Harris, where everywhere looked like a barren rocky moon landscape. Kirsten made her way to where she saw a large aerial off the road.

'It's just like the last one you went to, isn't it?'

'It's not far different. It's another aerial site, and we're going to stay inside for a while.' She took a left turn up a rocky track, was able to park the car out of sight of the road below behind a hut that served as the operating room for the aerial outside. Kirsten broke the lock, went inside, and ushered her two guests inside as well. There was a small heater inside, keeping the room at a constant temperature, and Kirsten knew at least the pair wouldn't freeze.

'I'm leaving you for a while, just going to check what's going on, but I'll be back. I'll try and bring some food this time.'

Kirsten drove back towards Leverburgh, picking up a few sandwiches and drinks from a small shop. She then made her way to the harbour, casually walking around it looking to see if there were any boats in the distance, but there were none. Anna hadn't texted yet, and she found herself struggling to find a phone signal, but when she did, nothing had come through. Reluctantly, Kirsten made her way back to the aerial site and delivered the food to Ollie and Innocence. Once they'd eaten, Kirsten had them stay there until darkness had fallen when she got them back in her car and drove out towards Leverburgh.

She parked and took the pair up the side of a hill looking down towards the harbour.

'We just wait here till we see something happening.'

'It's getting cold,' said Innocence, and Kirsten took off her jacket, wrapping it around the girl.

'Not long now, just hang in there,' said Kirsten. 'Hang on in there.'

Kirsten stood up, her eyes peeled out into the sound of Harris, and she saw a white light in the distance. A boat was coming towards them, and she stood there for half an hour watching it approach the harbour before mooring up. Taking her jacket back, Kirsten tapped Ollie on the shoulder, advising him to stay close to his sister. She made her way down the hillside onto the streets of Leverburgh.

Making her way over towards the harbour, Kirsten could feel her mobile phone vibrating. She picked it up to find a message saying, *Just arrived Leverburgh Harbour*. It seemed Anna Hunt had come through, or at least she was playing the part. It was quite a motivational speech the woman had made earlier on in the day. Kirsten was feeling generous towards her, but Anna had been right; you had to be careful who you trusted in this game, and you couldn't let your personal feelings drive your actions. You had to look at what was happening and that's what she would do now. She would scour around this vessel to make sure that nothing untoward was going to happen to Innocence and her brother.

Chapter 21

Kirsten could see the boat that was meant to pick her up in the harbour at Leverburgh. From the position up on the hill, she had noted that it seemed to be running smoothly. There was no one paying it any particular attention and there was nothing ostentatious about the boat. In fact, if anything, it seemed to just blend away. A basic fisher with a small deck on the back for casting, and a cockpit at the front. Down inside was an area to make teas and coffees, but there was nowhere in particular to sleep.

Anna must have been looking for a short route, and then to get away by some other method, thought Kirsten. It was unlikely that she would cross the Minch, the water between the island and the mainland, without some difficulty in something that small. Although it could be done, you'd have to hold on to your stomach.

Kirsten watched the boat alongside the harbour, and saw a man get out and begin to stretch his legs. He walked up and down, and then Kirsten noted that he made his way out for supplies, arriving at the little shop she had been in earlier that day. When he didn't come out from the shop, Kirsten made her way to the shop and entered.

Through the front door there were two main aisles stretching away, and then further aisles towards the rear of the shop. Food was stacked high, and there was a number of people in shopping for provisions. The nearest supermarket of mainland size was in Stornoway, although Tarbert, some forty-five minutes back up the road, did have a slightly larger shop. Hence the shop provided for the local area, and as Kirsten strolled down the aisle, she could see at the frozen food section the man who had exited the boat. He was reaching inside one of the cabinets. Kirsten took hold of the door he'd just opened, and closed it gently onto his arm, grabbing the man, but not in a violent way.

'I'm looking to book a sea passage.'

'Well, you'd better find somebody for hire then.'

'I always thought a little fisher would do.'

'Have you many passengers?' The man turned and stared at Kirsten.

'None, just bringing a couple of sprats with me.'

The man nodded, then leaned forward to whisper in Kirsten's ear. 'Forty-five minutes, just walk on and we leave.'

Kirsten let go of the door she was holding, nodded, and walked back down the aisle, picking up a can of Coke before making her way to the counter and paying for it. As she did so she got an uneasy feeling and thought a woman picking up bread from the aisle nearby was watching her intently. When Kirsten stared at her, the woman immediately looked away.

It was one of those things. If she'd been a spy trying to track Kirsten down, it was probably the last thing she should have done, simply look away. On the other hand, Kirsten never quite knew who she was dealing with. How good were the people coming to look for you? You had to be aware they came in all shapes and sizes, but so far there was nothing to say call the escape attempt off, and she exited, making her way along the road before cutting back up into the hills where Ollie and Innocence were hiding out in tall grass.

'Are we going to get to go?' asked Innocence.

'She's getting tired of this,' said Ollie. 'She can't take much more. We're just running here, there, and everywhere on these islands.'

'It's on,' said Kirsten, 'but that doesn't mean I can't call it off. You stay close and do what I say. We'll make a move in about half an hour.'

As they waited for the time to pass, a low mist began to set in and drizzle fell from the sky. Kirsten could feel herself getting wet and was glad when the half hour was up. So far, she'd observed very little down by the harbour; just the normal comings and goings, but that didn't mean there wasn't still danger. Kirsten took the young people back to her car, making them get into the boot before she drove into the harbour area.

The last run of the Leverburgh to Uist ferry had just arrived, and a number of cars got off, most driving away, but two remained around the car park area. Kirsten sat looking out at them, realising there were four men in each car. It wasn't often that that happened, although of course, it was always possible to have people travelling together, but it made Kirsten wary. She pulled her jacket around her shoulders, tucking her hair down behind inside her jacket.

Exiting her car, she walked down towards the ferry as if she was asking to get on. Stopping for a moment to talk about tickets and times of travel to the operative who was collecting tickets in from the cars lined up to make the journey back over to Uist, Kirsten asked rather mundane questions. She was ignoring the answers but instead looking around her, and she noticed that the four men had got out of the first car, while the other four remained.

Thanking the ticket collector, she walked over past the lifeboat station and onto the harbour. At the end of the pier, she saw the man she'd met in the supermarket, and he gave her a nod before disappearing down the small ladder towards his boat. Kirsten walked over to the edge, looked along, and got a thumbs up from the man through the screen of the tiny cockpit. Four men walked past behind Kirsten. As she looked out past the boats out to sea, she never flinched, but she was going to stay to see where they were going.

The men reached the end of the pier, then seemed to look around nonchalantly before one of them descended down the ladder towards the small boat. Kirsten watched from the corner of her eye and saw the fracas beginning inside the small boat. Immediately she was torn. If they made her car, the young people could be in danger. But this man who had come over on the boat was likely not going to be going anywhere else except to a wooden box in a graveyard.

Kirsten turned away and tried to nonchalantly move off the harbour wall to get a quick look at her car. It was still sitting in the same position, a car beyond with four men in it. What she should do as a spy was to simply walk away, take the young people with her and go and hide out again, because it seemed that this escape route had been busted. But Kirsten knew what was going to happen further down the pier, and so she turned around, walked back along the harbour wall, made her way slowly towards the two men at the top of the ladder.

'I'm afraid you can't come down here, miss. There's a little bit of trouble with a boat on this end. It'd be safer if you just left and got off the pier.'

Kirsten was walking forward with her head down, hair pulled out and hanging around her face. As she came closer, the man reiterated his words and stepped towards her.

'You can't come here, I said to you. There's trouble at this end of the pier, we're going to be closing it off soon. If you'd kindly just step away, we'll deal with it.'

'But all I wanted was a photograph from the end,' said Kirsten.

The man put both arms out. 'Look, love, you can't go this way.'

Kirsten grabbed his wrist. Before he realised what was happening, she'd spun the man and he'd gone off the harbour wall into the water below. His colleague tried to react, but Kirsten was already on her way to him, driving a knee up between his legs before hitting him with a forearm in the face. She punched several times before the man hit the floor. He tried to scramble back up, but she kicked him in the behind, causing him to roll, and then she kicked him again until he too tumbled off the harbour wall. She ran to the ladder but saw a man coming out of the wheelhouse of the boat.

The drop was a good ten feet but Kirsten didn't hesitate, jumping off and landing beside the man and then clattered into him, causing him to smack his head off the back lip of the boat. Kirsten had landed heavily on her feet but she shook her head briefly before looking into the cabin and seeing the man who would drive her away being stabbed in the shoulder.

Kirsten ran forward, grabbed the hand of the assailant, pulling it back, yanking hard down on the wrist and causing the hand to open, the knife tumbling to the floor. The man she had clattered into got back up on his feet. As he reached for the knife, she launched a kick into his face. After seeing him fall again, she turned back to the man who had attacked her pilot and spun him around in the tiny cabin. She pushed him up against the wall of the cockpit and hit him twice in the face with a punch.

Kirsten knew she needed to keep moving, keep everything at a pace and then get out of there before anybody knew what happened.

'Are you okay?' she asked the pilot of the boat.

'He stabbed me in the shoulder.'

'Can you use your arm, can you pilot this thing?'

'I think so.'

'Right, while I get out of here, you kick off. Just get clear.'

'But you're meant to be coming with me.'

'That's irrelevant. It's not safe anymore; they know about it. Just get clear.'

With that, Kirsten grabbed the man she had held up against the inside of the cockpit, then dragged him outside before throwing him off the boat. The man she kicked in the head was lying possibly unconscious but she grabbed him and tossed him off the boat anyway. There was no time for remorse, no time for looking after people who had come to kill her.

Quickly she climbed up the ladder, untying the little boat and watched as it began to make its way back out of the harbour. She saw the looks from a few other boats around her, still out moored away from the harbour wall, but she ignored any shouts and simply walked casually along the harbour pier before making her way back towards her car. She saw the four men still in the car and Kirsten got inside her own before driving off.

The car started up and followed her so instead of turning right from the harbour exit, she took a left instead, making her way along through Leverburgh before turning and parking up at a little house at the side of the road. Kirsten could see a car already inside the driveway and parked hers behind it. As she got out, she noted the other car with the four men in it was sitting at the roadside. Slowly she walked up to the front door and rang the bell. A man opened the door and gave a smile as he saw her. 'Can I help you?' he said.

'I'm sorry but my mobile has run out of charge,' said Kirsten. 'Do you mind if I come inside for a bit, and can I use your phone?'

'Well, it's a bit unusual,' said the man.

'I know, but I'm trying to arrange accommodation and I need to get somewhere tonight so if you don't mind.'

'Sure,' said the man. 'Come on in.' With that, Kirsten stepped up to the front door but then she grabbed him, planting a kiss on the man, wrapping her arms around him quickly.

When she broke off, she whispered in the man's ear. 'Just go with it. I've got a man following me. I think I'm in trouble.' The man she was holding immediately held even tighter and resumed the kiss. After a minute of holding each other, Kirsten turned, closed the door, and made sure that those outside could see her take the man's hand and start to walk him upstairs. When she got to the landing with the man, she told him to go into his bedroom, where she crouched down and went over to a window at the front of the house. Looking up, she saw the four men drive off.

'John. John, where are you?' Kirsten looked over the banister and saw a woman down below looking up at her.

'I'm up here, Annie.'

'Who the heck's that?' asked Annie.

Kirsten made her way to the stairs and began descending.

'I'm sorry to bother you. My name is Melinda, Melinda Jones and unfortunately, I've just had a rather nasty incident. I think somebody was trying to follow me off the boat.'

'Off the boat?' said Annie. 'That's terrible. And you think what, he was after you for what?'

'For a bit of you know what,' said Kirsten. 'But I see he's driven off, so thank you. I'm sorry to have bothered you.'

'Oh, it's been no trouble at all,' said John, smiling a little too much, Kirsten thought. 'You can stay for a cup of tea if you like,' said John. Kirsten looked at Annie and thought that tea wasn't really on offer.

'No, I better get going off to my own space but thank you again.'

'What did you say your name was again?' asked Annie.

'Melinda, Melinda Jones.'

'You really should report that sort of thing to the police.'

'I will do,' said Kirsten. 'But right now, I just want to go find my digs and have a shower. I'm sure you can understand that.'

Annie nodded. 'God love you. Take care. If you need anything else, you know, just say.'

'Absolutely,' said John. 'You need anything else, just come back.'

Kirsten caught the look from Annie to John. Coming back wasn't really on the cards. Maybe a phone call or a polite *never bother them again.*

'Well, thanks for your help,' said Kirsten, and made her way back to the car. She started it up, saying nothing until she had reversed it, and begun driving back into Leverburgh, before taking the road out towards the aerial mast where they'd previously hidden.

'Everybody okay in the back?'

'What's going on?' said Ollie.

'We got compromised.'

'Does that mean we're not going?' said Innocence.

'That's correct,' said Kirsten. 'We have to hide out and start again.'

She could hear Innocence begin to cry, and her brother consoling her, but inside Kirsten wondered what was really going on. How did something set up by Anna get compromised, and so easily? She needed to find out if Richard had been involved. She needed to call Anna.

Chapter 22

Kirsten arrived at the aerial site just along from Leverburgh they had occupied earlier on in the day. Having placed the two young people inside, she stepped outside and, using another of her SIM cards, she called Anna Hunt. She felt the rain drizzling on top of her. Looking out to sea, she could see little because it was dark and also because of the mist that was hanging around the island. Thankfully, it seemed the midge season was gone, because otherwise tonight would be a perfect night for them.

'It's Anna.'

'That was a bust. Someone there, eight of them. Lucky to get away without any casualties.'

'I hear there's a few casualties floating in the sea,' said Anna.

'Did your man get out?' asked Kirsten.

'Yeah, he's okay.'

'So how did we get caught?'

'I did this one by the book,' said Anna. 'But I never told Richard directly. I think he's clearly observing. But I'm not sure who's working with him. It seems an awful lot of organisation if somebody up above isn't involved too.

Otherwise, I'd bring him in right now.'

'What about me?' said Kirsten. 'What am I going to do with Innocence?'

'We're going to have to look elsewhere, outside of our own service, see who else I can contact and work with. Give me an hour, then call me back. If I haven't spoken to you within the hour, get on the move,' said Anna. 'Last thing you need to do is stay still anywhere. If you're in Leverburgh, they'll know you've been about, so they'll start hunting places.'

Kirsten thought she was fairly safe up at the aerial site, believing that nobody came here except for engineers wanting to check the aerial. But maybe Anna was right. She had more experience at this than Kirsten did.

Kirsten waited outside in the rain, making sure no one came up the path towards the little hut that held all the electrical equipment for the aerial. On a nice day, it was a rather spectacular sight to see this aerial reaching up to the skies. Maybe not as impressive as the first one she'd had cause to go to at Forsnaval, but all the same, amongst this rocky outcrop towards the east side of Harris, it had something of a lunar quality about it. Kirsten waited until an hour had gone before calling Anna Hunt again.

'What's the deal, Anna?' asked Kirsten.

'I've been in contact with another government organisation,' she said. 'I'm not saying who in case anyone picks up this call. But look for the three lights at Luskentyre, that's your shelter. They'll also tell you further. And good luck, Kirsten. It seems to be a lot bigger than what I thought.'

Kirsten closed the call, but she could feel her hands begin to shake. She'd never heard Anna talk like this, something being bigger than her. Clearly, something was gravely amiss further up the service. But there was no time to think about that now. Instead, she headed back inside the little hut and stood looking at Ollie, holding his sister. The girl was asleep at the moment and Ollie's face was looking deeply pained.

'Are we on the move again?' he asked.

'Yes. Hopefully somewhere safe, and then on a bit further.'

'What if Innocence just told him she wouldn't testify?'

'Wouldn't work, Ollie. I'm sorry, but your sister's caught up in this now. He would never take her word for it. Collins, the man she saw murder someone, he couldn't take the risk she'd ever renege on that. He's coming for her. Until she actually testifies, there is not a lot for her. We need to get you into witness relocation. We need to get you away, all of you.'

'I don't want to go away. I'm happy where I am,' said Ollie.

'It's a rubbish deal,' said Kirsten, 'and I can't change that. All I can do is keep you safe.'

'What happened down at the harbour? I wasn't able to hear much in the boot of the car.'

'Eight men came, I managed to throw four of them off our tail. A few others are out in the sea. The guy who came to give you a hand, take you away in his boat, he got a knife in the shoulder for his troubles. I hope you're seeing it, Ollie. There is no safe place back in Inverness. To be safe, you have to be away. You have to become unknown to people.'

Kirsten asked Ollie to carry Innocence into the rear of the car and he laid her in the back seat while he laid down in the well between the front and rear seats. Kirsten drove the car past the long expanses of water outside of Leverburgh before making her way down towards Luskentyre. As the car came over a hill, she spotted three torchlights all close together being shone towards her briefly for a moment, and then they disappeared.

She continued down along the road before taking a left past one of the glorious beaches. As she drove along, suddenly, a man stepped out in front of her, holding two hands up to the air. Kirsten stopped the car, kept her lights on him so he was blinded, while she opened the door. Taking out her gun, she pointed it at him.

'Speak quick,' she said.

'Five houses down, on the left, key under the porch mat. Anna sends her compliments.' Unflustered, the man walked away back into the darkness.

Kirsten jumped back in the car and continued to drive before turning in at a small white cottage at the side of the loch. With the car parked up, she stepped out, took the key, and searched the house from top to bottom. Once she was satisfied that there was no one about, Kirsten brought her charges inside the house, allowing Ollie to take his sister upstairs, where they both fell asleep on the bed. Kirsten made herself a coffee and sat downstairs looking at the large windows. She thought she could make out in the distance a couple of figures, but this would be Anna and her crew protecting the house quietly.

There came a knock at the backdoor, and with her gun, Kirsten slowly made her way round before she saw Anna Hunt's face at the door. Opening it cautiously, she let her boss into the kitchen.

'You can ease down,' said Anna. 'I've got people all round here, not from our department. You're going to need to sleep.'

'Why? What are we doing?' asked Kirsten.

'We need to get her off this island, for a start. If we can get her to the mainland I can get her in a convoy, get her away somewhere safe. Very safe. Far end of the country, safe. Military base if we have to.'

177

'Okay, but how are we going to do that?' asked Kirsten.

'I'm trusting no one. These guys have been good, but when I want her gone, I don't want any leads back to her. I have my contact to hand over to and then we're done. It's with other departments.'

'And you know they're good?'

'I know they're good. Look, Kirsten, we've got something wrong in our department and I'm going to rain fire on it, but for the moment, our top priority is to get this girl out of here. I've been able to get her father, her mother and her brother and sister on their way already. There's only these two to get safe. I've gone incommunicado as well, and that goes for me and you. I'll be here tomorrow round about ten o'clock. We're going to get the small ferry over to Uist and from there, we'll get to Lochmaddy and then on to Skye. Someone will meet us there. If anything happens to me, you're looking for the man with the black hat.'

Kirsten laughed. 'The man in the black hat. It's all very spy-thriller, isn't it?'

'Sorry,' said Anna. 'But yes, it is. We're also being very careful because while our department's compromised, who knows who Collins has elsewhere.'

'Why are you doing this on your own? It's not like you to step back into the field,' said Kirsten. Anna gave her a look.

'I've always told you I was a field operative. I know how to get things done. Frankly, if I don't clean house, my career's over. There's a trail of bodies going back, with a lot of answers being looked for. If we don't get it sorted, they'll scape goat whoever was in charge. Don't worry, you'll be okay. After all, you were the one facing the bullets, but I'm running the op. Frankly, they don't take kindly when they go this awry.'

'It's not awry yet,' said Kirsten. 'If we get them there, she testifies, it'll still be a big coup. All the more so for having made it work.'

'You say that, but I'm going to have to bring Samantha in. She let the father and the elder son go. Of course, she did. That was how they were hoping to flush out Innocence, find her, but you did well, Kirsten. You got there, and you kept getting there. Just one more stint for the pair of us. I'll be here tomorrow with a camper van. We go over to Uist on the small ferry; we then get the larger ferry. Lochmaddy over to Uig, drop them off with the man in the black hat.'

'All sounds very simple,' said Kirsten.

'It does, doesn't it? Like something you can make up on a sheet of paper. How simple has it been for you so far?' Anna give a wry smile. 'Look, we haven't always seen eye to eye, and I probably didn't treat you that well last time, when you stopped the gunman with the first minister, but tomorrow it's you and me. Until we get to the man with a black hat, it's just you and me. Just make sure you're ready. That's why I want you to get a good night's sleep.'

'What about you?' asked Kirsten. 'Are you going to sleep as well?'

'I need to clear house,' said Anna. 'Got things to organise, but I'll be here and I'll be ready. Don't worry about that. Good night, Stewart. I'll see you tomorrow.' With that, Anna slid out the back door, and after a few moments, Kirsten found it difficult to keep track of her movements as she disappeared off in the dark.

Kirsten didn't sleep particularly well. Instead, she sat in an armchair downstairs with a gun in her hand. For all Anna's assurances of how the other government agency was

179

protecting them, she wasn't going to go this far and then give up her charges. Besides, there was still that nagging doubt that Anna had something to do with this. Kirsten had to play the facts, not the feelings, and at the moment, she didn't know a lot about anyone, but this would prove it with Anna. Kirsten wasn't looking forward to the idea that Anna may not be all she said she was.

If she was actually one of the perpetrators of this action against Innocence, then maybe she would be taking a payday and running after doing the deed. If she wasn't, then they were in trouble from other sources, especially if Anna felt the need to go incommunicado.

The sun rose, having driven away a misty night, and Kirsten looked out along the glorious water of Luskentyre. She could see the beaches stretching out, and kicked herself for never having come here during her time when she was working at the police station in Stornoway. She had been here, but only on duty.

Oliver and Innocence awoke just after seven a.m., and Kirsten took them breakfast up, cereal that was in the cupboard. She'd found long-life milk as well, and made sure that everyone was well fed before Anna's arrival. The camper van pulled up on the road outside and Kirsten quickly ran the brother and sister towards it, stowing them into the rear of it before Anna drove off.

As they arrived at Leverbrugh, Kirsten opened up compartments within the camper van, and managed to hide Innocence and Oliver over inside them. Anna got into the rear, and then satisfied that the pair were well hidden, she asked Kirsten to come and sit in the front with her.

'Eyes and ears, Kirsten. Eyes and ears. They may come for

us at any time.'

The small ferry over to Uist was an open affair, roll on and roll off. From her position in the cabin at the top of the ferry, Kirsten could see down onto the deck, and positioned herself to be able to see anyone moving towards the camper van. If need be, she could make a shot from there, but her gun was well hidden. Anna was regularly standing up, walking around, and checking everyone who was on board. Yet Kirsten knew that she was doing it in the most amicable way, saying hello to everyone as she passed them by.

On exiting the ferry, they drove the short distance down to Lochmaddy to await the next ferry out towards the Isle of Skye and Uig. The ferry trip would be only an hour and a half, and then they'd be there, ready to hand over their prize. But something was bothering Kirsten as she sat awaiting the ferry, looking at the cars around her. Maybe it was the different accents she was hearing. In summer you would've heard a number of localities expressed in the language around, but coming into winter, more and more of the passengers onboard were simply from the island. But Kirsten heard more voices than she expected to, with either a mainland brogue or even those with an English accent.

All of them seemed fine. There was an older couple making their way home, or so it seemed. Tradesmen, coming back and forward. Maybe it was just a sign of the changing times of the island, that nowadays there was fewer and fewer of local voices, but it made Kirsten jumpy. When Anna got in and started up the vehicle to board the ferry, Kirsten remembered being attacked on the ferry over to Stornoway.

As they drove onboard, the camper van bouncing about until it settled down into its parking area, Kirsten caught the eye of

Anna, who was looking from wing mirror to wing mirror.
'Eyes and ears, Stewart. Let's keep the lookout.'

Chapter 23

Kirsten stepped out of the camper van and wanted to give a tap on the side to indicate to Innocence and Ollie that everything was okay, but she refrained, knowing that eyes could be on her at the moment. Eyes could be anywhere looking for them.

Anna Hunt had done a good job of disguising herself, and one would've barely recognised her looking more like a Romany traveller than a hard-nosed smart manager of spies. Around her head, she wore a headscarf and had an earring hanging from her left ear the size of a small ball. Her clothing was far less official. She seemed to be wrapped up in folds of cloth that never seemed to end. She struck a funny figure beside Kirsten's black outfit, but Kirsten didn't care. The woman obviously had some knowledge about what to do in these situations and she was carrying out things to the best of her ability.

One thing that was bothering Kirsten was that as passengers, they'd have to make their way onto the upper decks, and unlike the Loch Seaforth Stornoway ferry, she wouldn't find a seat with a view of the car deck.

'We're just going to have to take it in turns. Watch the doors as well.'

'Or, one of us could just stay here with the camper van,' said Kirsten.

'No way. Dead giveaway,' said Anna. 'If somebody clocks us on board, they're not necessarily going to know what vehicle we're in, or indeed, if we've left anybody there unless they've watched us the whole time through. Frankly, if they've got eyes on already, we could be in trouble.'

Kirsten gave a brief nod and then looked over laughing and mentioned that they really needed to get up onto the upper deck. Together they made their way to the stairwell, but at the top, Anna Hunt waited while Kirsten went off to find a seat. She made her way through to the cafeteria area and took up a seat beside the window. It would not be long before they were underway. She wondered if maybe that was when the deed would be done. Although if they did try to kill them, how would they get off? Surely the most dangerous times would be before the ferry got underway and as it was just arriving in Uig. That was when escape for the attackers would be most accessible.

Kirsten watched the water churn down below as the ferry moved off its berth and started to make way to the open sea. Within five minutes of the doors being closed up and being underway, Anna Hunt appeared and sat down opposite Kirsten and told her to go for a walk, making sure she went past all the entrances to the car deck. Kirsten acknowledged the sense of this and began to purposefully wander around. When she returned twenty minutes later, sitting opposite Anna Hunt, the woman was holding her hands out four fingers on each hand, the thumbs tucked underneath her palms. Something was up. Kirsten leaned forward.

'Richard's here. He's in the bar.'

Kirsten's face sunk; so, he was onto them.

'I'm going to get on the move around the vessel, pick out who his people are. I don't think he'll see me coming, but either way, I don't want you too far away, so follow me, but at a distance. I'll shout if anything's happening.'

Kirsten nodded and waited for her boss to stand up from the table and begin her walk around the ferry. It wasn't the largest ferry in the world by any stretch of the imagination and Kirsten wondered what justification she could have for wandering while she made her way about. As she strolled along, she felt the gun sitting just behind her hip, and she wondered if she'd have to use it again.

Something flashed in her mind. The first time she had shot someone was protecting two tourists in a camper van. Kirsten had brought the fight to them and had reluctantly pulled her gun to shoot down two men who were hunting Kirsten down. It had affected her, and she'd been through counselling since, but it wasn't something she took to with any sense of pleasure. She would rather avoid killing people if she could get away with it, but it seemed protecting Innocence meant she had to give up her own.

Kirsten was now on a passageway down to the bar area but turned and began to read some information about the ferry that was framed on the wall. Numbers swam before her eyes, but she was screening with her ears, listening as intently as she could to anything from inside the bar. It was five minutes later when Anna Hunt walked past carrying a coffee. As she brushed past Kirsten, there came a faint whisper, 'At least five, maybe six.'

Kirsten could feel herself shake. The trouble was you never knew quite how good others were until you took them on in combat. Richard would know his stuff and maybe this time he brought people who also knew it. Were there no quality thugs on the island? Was that why they were so poor at handling the situation?

Kirsten made her way back to the cafe, sat down in front of Anna Hunt who briefly gave a description of each of the men that she had seen. 'That might not be all of them though,' said Anna, 'and don't be afraid to look for women either.'

'There's no need to teach me to suck eggs,' said Kirsten. 'I am aware of what I'm doing. I've kept the girl alive for this long.'

'Let's hope we can do it for the next half hour because that's when we'll be docking; until then, we need to keep on the move. Keep close to the doors.'

Kirsten got up and began to wander the ship again, but as she passed several of the luggage racks, she saw a man matching the description that Anna had given. He went to make his way down the stairwell and Kirsten bumped into him.

'Oh, sorry,' said Kirsten. 'Are you going down there? I didn't think we were allowed to do that. I could get one of the crew for you if you want.' Kirsten saw his hand go for where a holster would be and struck out instantly, catching the man under the throat with a jab of her hand. She heard him gurgle, but then something hit her across the back.

She fell to her knees, but instead of turning around to face who was there, she rolled to one side as grasping hands reached down for her. Turning, she saw three men. The first man was pulling a gun out and Kirsten lashed a kick that caught his hand, dropping the gun down. She reached down for her own weapon, but the men moved forward and she felt hands grasp her.

She struggled, throwing her weight this way and that,

bouncing off the walls of the ferry. The corridor was tight. While she was grappling with three of them, she heard a laugh from behind her. She briefly saw the face of Richard as she started to descend the stairs down to the car deck.

'Anna,' shouted, Kirsten, 'Anna, he's making his move.'

A hand clamped over her mouth, but Kirsten bit it. She felt another punch to the head and had that claustrophobic feeling she always felt when she'd been jumped in the mixed martial arts matches she took part in. There, she'd be pressed down on the floor, only to wrap up to prevent people striking her at the head, struggling for a way out. This time she was taking a kicking in the sides as she went down to the floor.

Covering her head, her eyes looked up and saw a fire extinguisher in front of her. Quickly she reached for it, pulling it off its mount. It fell onto the foot of the man in front of her. He yelled and Kirsten reached forward, biting into his leg. Behind her, she kicked as hard as she could as the others tried to fall on top of her. Rolling on her back, she was able to kick out hard, catching one under the chin.

The next one hovered over her, ready to strike. She reached up, punching him right between the legs, causing him to double over in agony. She stumbled away, getting up to her feet, but then realised if any of them reached for a gun, she was an easy target in this corridor. She ran forward, barrelling into them again, but her force didn't carry her far enough. The men were still standing and put another hand upon her. Kirsten kicked again but saw the man at the rear pull the gun.

'Get out of the way. I'll take the bitch down.'

Kirsten turned, fled, and as she believed the man would be ready to shoot, she flung herself on the floor. Her timing was good, and the shot disappeared over her head before she was up again and raced behind a seat.

There was chaos on the ferry now, and people shouting and yelling, scrambling to get away from the area. Kirsten cut into a little side corridor but stopped, letting some passengers race past before she pulled out her gun. As the first man arrived, she shot him straight in the stomach and watched him double over. She then peered out quickly looking back down the corridor, but the men, having seen their friend drop, had sought cover for themselves.

Kirsten made her way into the galley off a door behind her, and her gun caused panic amongst the kitchen staff.

'Special agent,' shouted Kirsten. 'I'm with the government. How do I get to the car deck?'

No one responded, instead they started screaming and began to run. Kirsten grabbed one of the chefs by the collar and hauled him towards her face. 'How do I get to the car deck?'

'Through there,' he said, pointing to a fire door. 'Take a right then take a left, down and through the crew quarters. If you keep going down, there'll be a door at the bottom.' Kirsten nodded but heard the door behind her open. She spun quickly, weapon up, saw the face of one of the men who had attacked, and fired. He catapulted backwards but jammed the door open with his body.

'Get out of here,' said Kirsten. 'Go and hide.' With that, she ran for the door beyond. She heard it close behind her before several shots pinged off it. *This is a bloody mess. Richard must really be desperate if he's got guns going off on a ferry*. The man must have realised this was his last chance.

Kirsten made her way down through crew quarters, and as she saw a couple of doors opening up, she raised her gun, shouting at people to get back in their rooms and lock the doors.

'Don't come out whatever you do. Do not come out until someone comes for you.' She found the stairs and continued down until eventually, she found a door leading onto the car deck. It was marked as such but for staff only. Pressing one of the buttons, it opened, sliding to the left.

Richard's face was revealed on the far side of the deck across a few cars, and Kirsten had only a moment to react before he raised his gun and fired it at her. She spun inside behind the door, and when she peered back out, he was gone. Rather than stay put, she knelt down behind the car and began to look about, trying to orientate herself with where she was on the vessel. As she stopped, hiding behind the large Mercedes, she saw the headscarf of Anna Hunt moving behind the car across from her.

From the door behind Anna, she saw a man emerge, gun raised, and he tore off between several cars after Anna. Kirsten didn't wait. Scrambling along behind the cars, she found the line she wanted in between several of them and fired at the man. She watched him slump down, saw Anna turn but quickly make her way in behind other cars.

Anna had said six, thought Kirsten. *I've shot one up top, that's two. Three others plus Richard if the others are still in any state.* She made her way across and stood beside the door the man had come out of. Ten seconds later, another man emerged but Kirsten grabbed his head, instantly driving it down into one of the cars. The man bounced and fell to the floor, out cold.

Kirsten peered inside the door, then up the stairwell but saw no one else. Making her way back out onto the car deck, she saw another door open on the far side from where she'd emerged previously. Quickly, she knelt down. The man began to make his way towards the middle of the vessel right where the camper van was. As he reached the back door, Kirsten could hear a scream. Innocence must have been spooked by the gunfire.

Kirsten saw the man raise his weapon to start firing inside the vehicle. Jumping up onto the roof of a car, Kirsten fired at him once just to the left, which caused the man to turn and look at her. The second time caught him in the shoulder, and he fell to the ground. Then, the windows of the car Kirsten was standing on blew out at a shot having been sent from somewhere else.

One more in the mix, thought Kirsten, *one more*, but she also knew now that the caravan had been identified and started making her way off the car and down behind vehicles. She spun around a blue Volkswagen and ran straight into another man with a red hat on. She was about to fire when she recognised him as crew.

'Get down. Get under that car. Do not move,' said Kirsten. The man looked at the gun and did instantly what she'd said. A shot rang out over the top of her, and Kirsten could feel the ferry begin to swing. It must be coming in close to the Uig. She worked her away underneath another car, looking for feet, and saw someone else moving about three cars away. She rolled out, casually looked up through the windscreens of the car, and saw the shadow moving in towards the camper van.

Kirsten stood up and the man saw her as well, but she was able to fire several times catching him on the shoulder. He seemed to be still moving, so she ran across the back of the camper van making her way towards the body that had hit the ground. Sure enough, his arms were still moving, and he was raising his weapon as she fired. Forcing back her disgust at

190

the damage her gun had done, Kirsten looked left and right before she heard somebody behind her.

'So near yet so far, Kirsten. Sad to see you go.'

Kirsten spun round and there was Richard pointing a gun right at her. There was no time to move, no time to do anything else. She was gone.

And then she saw him tumble off to the side, bouncing off a car as his head half exploded. Something within Kirsten jumped, something struggling with the scene before her, and she began to shake realising she'd been moments from death. As she stood there quivering, Anna Hunt emerged from behind the camper van. Her scarf was now off her head, and her hair began shaking out. She looked down with contempt at the body of the man in front of her.

'It's my section. Do you hear? My section!' The woman spat at the corpse. 'We don't do traitors!' With that, Anna looked across at Kirsten. 'All done,' she said.

Kirsten looked around her. 'Good job they are,' but Kirsten knew that Anna was well aware of the situation.

'Are you okay?'

Kirsten looked at Anna and shook her head. 'No, but let's get on. They're not going to let us drive off here now, are they? Bodies everywhere.'

'No, but we take them up top, we'll be first off this ferry.'

Kirsten nodded, unlocked the camper van, and announced to Ollie and Innocence that they were safe. She opened the door, found their hidey-hole, and opened it. The girl was shaking and was white. Ollie wasn't looking very good too, and when he climbed out of the campervan, he vomited onto the floor of the ferry.

'Let's get going,' said Anna Hunt, and with Anna in the lead,

Kirsten followed her all the way up through the crew quarters until they reached the bridge of the vessel. When they came up on deck, the captain was going ballistic, but Anna pulled out a card, said who she was and what was going to happen. The man hesitated at first but when Anna spoke to the police he was now in consultation with and gave a code, they told him to do whatever she asked. Ten minutes later, Anna was at the head, Innocence and Ollie behind, and Kirsten walked down a gangplank and out onto a harbour side. There was a minibus waiting with darkened windows in the rear and Kirsten saw two women and two men waiting to take custody of her charges.

'Time to go,' said Anna, looking at Innocence and Ollie. 'They'll take care of you. You need to get somewhere safe.' Ollie stuck out a hand, shaking Anna's, and then turned and nodded at Kirsten. Innocence wasn't in any frame of mind and simply stumbled towards the minibus. She suddenly turned and ran back to Kirsten throwing her arms around her.

'You can't leave me. You've kept me safe till now; you can't leave.'

'I have to. You'll be okay now; you're in a much better place.'

Gently, Kirsten urged the girl into the minibus. As soon as she was inside, the doors were promptly closed, and the minibus sped off. Kirsten noticed several other cars departing at the same time and recognised a Protection Unit when she saw one. As she watched the minibus depart, she could see nothing through the windows and realised that that was the last view she would ever have of Innocence.

'There's going to be a ton of paperwork with this one,' said Anna, 'but you need to go somewhere for a rest. I can handle this. Why don't you disappear, and I'll see you in Inverness tomorrow.'

'Are you sure?' said Kirsten.

'Of course, I am. It's my department. It's what I do. Besides, after getting her through this, I think things will look up for us. Go on. Get yourself away.'

Kirsten nodded and made her way off the harbour side. It was there that she stopped and looked around her. *Get myself away*, she thought. *I'm in Uig on the Isle of Skye. The next bus probably isn't for an hour.* Turning around, she saw Anna Hunt's face creased in laughter.

'Get your arse back here. We've got work to do.'

Chapter 24

Anna Hunt had not been joking when she'd said there was work to do, and Kirsten spent the next month filling out reports and attending various committees where she explained different actions she had taken. There was a shake-up throughout the entire department, and it seemed that Richard had not been working alone. Higher up, even above Anna's pay grade, several figures tumbled. They couldn't prove everything they did, but there was enough suspicion with several of them that they were out, and never again would they be part of anything to do with law enforcement or protection of the country or individuals. Anna seemed to glory in all of it, and hers was the name touted with having chased out the rats in the department. Kirsten was surprised when Anna constantly held Kirsten up as being the one who protected Innocence.

The trial of Kyle Collins for the murder of Johnny Kerr would not be taking place for some time, but in the meantime, Collins was off the street placed into custody and refused bail until that time arrived. Anna consistently talked about how much of a win this was, and unachievable without her department despite what had gone on within it. Everyone was tenacious in fighting for it, keen for it to stay afloat, but the odds were against them, as she disappeared into sub-committee meetings, one after another to argue the department's case.

By this point with the reports all done, Kirsten had returned to Inverness. At first, there was so little going on she decided to take a two-week holiday, which involved a weekend spent lying around and licking her wounds, and then a trip to a mixed martial arts competition, where she was able to watch people who truly understood the game display their wares.

On her first day back in Inverness, the weather was grey and dull, and winter was just around the corner. Autumn, having truly arrived, detached leaves from trees, leaving them littering the streets, but there was a gorgeous golden hue to it.

Kirsten knew her way up the old stairs and went to step into her office when she came to be aware that the door was not closed in the fashion that she would normally have it. Instead, it was lying open slightly and that told her someone was inside. As she pushed the door back, she saw a smart set of heels, not too high, possibly okay to be run on, and with those heels came a set of legs she'd identify anywhere. Anna Hunt wasn't the most glamorous person, but her legs looked like a dancer's. She had strong thighs and the woman certainly kept in shape. Anna was wearing a black skirt this time with a black jacket over it and had glasses on, cutting the most serious of looks.

'Glad you're back; there's been a few developments.'

'Developments?' said Kirsten. 'We tied up that case, how could there be anything after that today?'

'Not with the case, with the department. You're now the new section head of the north.'

Kirsten stopped. 'No,' said Kirsten, 'that's your job.'

'No, it's not. I'm overall in Scotland, moved up a bit, and I've decided to rearrange things. You've got everything from Perth up. You'll run the ops, you'll run the intelligence, you'll be the one in charge.'

Kirsten looked around the room; it was just her there. 'That's quite a big job for someone on her own.'

'That it is,' said Anna, and stood up motioning for Kirsten to follow her. She opened the door, made her way across the badly-carpeted hallway, and opened another door into what would be the conference room. Sitting down at the far end was someone Kirsten recognised.

'You cannot be serious,' said Kirsten. From the far end of the table, Justin Chivers waved.

'You have my express permission to take him outside and boot him in the balls if he tries any of that sexist bollocks,' said Anna. 'But other than that, you're getting somebody I trust as much as anyone in that department, even as much as you.' Kirsten was quite taken aback, but Justin grinned.

'You're looking well,' said Justin. 'How far is that tan?' Kirsten put her finger up, 'Stop. You heard what the boss said, and I intend to carry that out.'

Justin smirked. Then he looked around. 'When are the rest arriving?'

'The rest?' asked Kirsten. 'What do you mean by that?'

'The rest of the team. Hasn't Anna told you?'

Kirsten looked at Anna who smiled before sitting down. 'If you're going to run the north, you're going to need a team under you. I suggest the next couple of weeks you and Justin get together, start picking your candidates.'

'So, what, run some advertisements?'

'No,' said Anna. 'Did we advertise for you? Like heck we did. We went and got you, and that's what you need to do. Talk to

Justin, he'll come up with profiles, details about anyone. That's what he's good at. You're not going to run as I ran. This is one tight unit taking care of the north, reporting in to me. You're going to be much more hands-on than I ever was.'

'Is there not anybody a bit more qualified than this?' asked Kirsten. 'I mean, I've only just joined the service really.'

'You're loyal,' said Anna, 'and you're smart. You kept that girl alive, and at times, I have no idea how in God's name you did it. I want you to pick who's coming, not me. I chose Richard. Next time I won't be choosing alone.'

'You chose me though,' said Kirsten. 'It wasn't all bad.'

'You chose me,' said Justin Chivers. Both women looked at him, daggers for eyes. 'Just saying, quite clever with a computer.'

Kirsten laughed. 'So, when do we start?' she asked Anna.

'Well, there's no time like the present. Like I said, spend a week finding who you want, spend the week after getting them. After that, you're live. Oh, and one other thing.'

'What?' asked Kirsten.

'Whenever you choose people and whatever you do, no one knows. You can't go and tell anyone as much as you want to.'

Kirsten nodded and took the hand of Anna Hunt as she extended it shaking it. 'Welcome, new section chief. Just make sure you do a good job,' said Anna, then she left, not once looking back. Kirsten turned around and looked at Justin Chivers at the end of the table.

'I'm just going out for a few minutes to let this soak in.'

Justin looked at her strangely, 'Are you sure you don't want someone to celebrate with?'

'No and remember the alleyway and what can happen. Start drawing up some names, people you think are assets we can use. I'll discuss it further with Anna.'

Kirsten made her way down the stairs and back out of the building before catching the bus further into town. She jumped off and made a phone call asking an old colleague if he was free for a coffee. When he said yes, Kirsten made her way inside one of the coffee shops, ordered, and sat down awaiting his arrival.

The day was busy. It was some twenty minutes before a familiar face walked in the door wearing a dark suit, a white shirt, and tie. Her old boss, Seoras Macleod, sat down in front of her. Kirsten said nothing until the coffee arrived. Then she sat in silence watching his quizzical face.

'What did you drag me out here for?' he asked. 'I appreciate the coffee, but why am I getting coffee?'

'I can't say,' said Kirsten.

'Right, so I take it things are going well.'

'I can't say,' said Kirsten.

'Then I'm a little bit bemused,' said Macleod.

'Thanks for looking after my brother.'

'I only pop in at times to see him.'

Kirsten's brother was in the home, suffering from a form of dementia. With her detail in the service, she rarely got to see him. Macleod, however, visited him religiously.

'You don't have to buy me coffee to do this. It's a pleasure.'

'Oh, no,' said Kirsten, 'the coffee is not for that; the coffee is for this.' She held up her cup indicating Macleod to do the same. 'To me,' she said.

'To you,' said Macleod. 'Now, what's this all about?'

'Can't say,' said Kirsten and sat and drank her coffee quickly before putting it on the table. 'Thank you,' she said. 'Thank you, inspector.'

'For what?'

'Everything.' With that, Kirsten gave him a hug before walking out of the coffee house.

The End

Read on to discover the Patrick Smythe series!

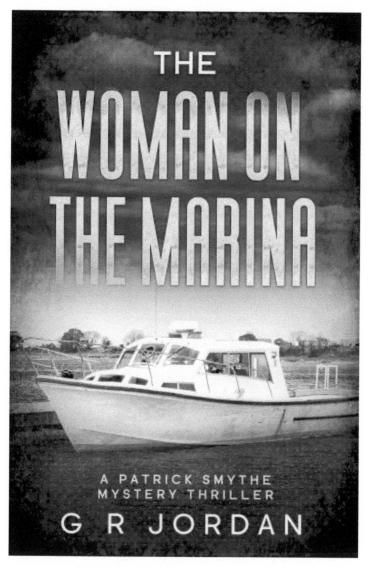

Start your Patrick Smythe journey here!

Patrick Smythe is a former Northern Irish policeman who

after suffering an amputation after a bomb blast, takes to the sea between the west coast of Scotland and his homeland to ply his trade as a private investigator. Join Paddy as he tries to work to his own ethics while knowing how to bend the rules he once enforced. Working from his beloved motorboat 'Craigantlet', Paddy decides to rescue a drug mule in this short story from the pen of G R Jordan.

Join G R Jordan's monthly newsletter about forthcoming releases and special writings for his tribe of avid readers and then receive your free Patrick Smythe short story.

Go to https://bit.ly/PatrickSmythe for your Patrick Smythe journey to start!

About the Author

GR Jordan is a self-published author who finally decided at forty that in order to have an enjoyable lifestyle, his creative beast within would have to be unleashed. His books mirror that conflict in life where acts of decency contend with self-promotion, goodness stares in horror at evil, and kindness blindsides us when we at our worst. Corrupting our world with his parade of wondrous and horrific characters, he highlights everyday tensions with fresh eyes whilst taking his methodical, intelligent mainstays on a roller-coaster ride of dilemmas, all the while suffering the banter of their provoca-tive sidekicks.

A graduate of Loughborough University where he masquer-aded as a chemical engineer but ultimately played American football, Gary had worked at changing the shape of cereal flakes and pulled a pallet truck for a living. Watching vegetables freeze at -40'C was another career highlight and he was also one of the Scottish Highlands "blind" air traffic controllers.

These days he has graduated to answering a telephone to people in trouble before telephoning other people to sort it out.

Having flirted with most places in the UK, he is now based in the Isle of Lewis in Scotland where his free time is spent between raising a young family with his wife, writing, figuring out how to work a loom and caring for a small flock of chickens. Luckily, his writing is influenced by his varied work and life experience as the chickens have not been the poetical inspiration he had hoped for!

You can connect with me on:

🌐 https://grjordan.com

🅵 https://facebook.com/carpetlessleprechaun

Subscribe to my newsletter:

✉ https://bit.ly/PatrickSmythe

Also by G R Jordan

G R Jordan writes across multiple genres including crime, dark and action adventure fantasy, feel good fantasy, mystery thriller and horror fantasy. Below is a selection of his work. Whilst all books are available across online stores, signed copies are available at his personal shop.

 **The Express Wishes of Mr MacIver (Kirsten Stewart Thrillers #3)**
https://grjordan.com/product/express-wishes
A scramble for diamonds on Scotland's north coast. A murderous group intent on an explosive end if disappointed. Can Kirsten prevent a catastrophe on the largest cruise ship to visit the Hebridean Isles?

In her third novel, Kirsten must use the guile and expertise of her newly formed team to prevent the largest shipping disaster ever seen in the northern waters of Scotland. With the clock ticking and a nation with its finger on the trigger, will the Inverness team find a country's missing heritage, or will they join thousands in an explosion of titanic proportions?

The cold waters of the Minch await the tardy courier!

The Culling at Singing Sands (Highlands & Islands Detective Book 15)

https://grjordan.com/product/the-culling-at-singing-sands

A glamorous retirement village on an isolated island. A brutal killer culls the elderly starting with the oldest resident. Can Macleod discover the murderous motive and prevent the island graveyard from overflowing?

When the Isle of Eigg enjoys the opening of 'The Singing Sands' Later but Better Township', little do they realise that death is only round the corner for the new arrivals. Joy turns to sorrow as old friends meet a bloody end, and DI Macleod and DS McGrath are dispatched to investigate. As a determined clientele and some unseasonal weather hamper the investigation, the detectives must look to the past to prevent the dispatching of those seen to be past their time.

Even in paradise you're only one step from the grave!

Corpse Reviver (A Contessa Munroe Mystery #1)

https://grjordan.com/product/corspe-reviver

A widowed Contessa flees to the northern waters in search of adventure. An entrepreneur dies on an ice pack excursion. But when the victim starts moonlighting from his locked cabin, can the Contessa uncover the true mystery of his death?

Catriona Cullodena Munroe, widow of the late Count de Los Palermo, has fled the family home, avoiding the scramble for title and land. As she searches for the life she always wanted, the Contessa, in the company of the autistic and rejected Tiff, must solve the mystery of a man who just won't let his business go.

Corpse Reviver is the first murder mystery involving the formidable and sometimes downright rude lady of leisure and her straight talking niece. Bonded by blood, and thrown together by fate, join this pair of thrill seekers as they realise that flirting with danger brings a price to pay.

Highlands and Islands Detective Thriller Series
https://grjordan.com/product/waters-edge

Join stalwart DI Macleod and his burgeoning new DC McGrath as they look into the darker side of the stunningly scenic and wilder parts of the north of Scotland. From the Black Isle to Lewis, from Mull to Harris and across to the small Isles, the Uists and Barra, this mismatched pairing follow murders, thieves and vengeful victims in an effort to restore tranquillity to the remoter parts of the land.

Be part of this tale of a surprise partnership amidst the foulest deeds and darkest souls who stalk this peaceful and most beautiful of lands, and you'll never see the Highlands the same way again

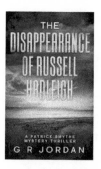

The Disappearance of Russell Hadleigh (Patrick Smythe Book 1)
https://grjordan.com/product/the-disappearance-of-russell-hadleigh
A retired judge fails to meet his golf partner. His wife calls for help while running a fantasy play ring. When Russians start co-opting into a fairly-traded clothing brand, can Paddy untangle the strands before the bodies start littering the golf course?

In his first full novel, Patrick Smythe, the single-armed former policeman, must infiltrate the golfing social scene to discover the fate of his client's husband. Assisted by a young starlet of the greens, Paddy tries to understand just who bears a grudge and who likes to play in the rough, culminating in a high stakes showdown where lives are hanging by the reaction of a moment. If you love pacey action, suspicious motives and devious characters, then Paddy Smythe operates amongst your kind of people.

Love is a matter of taste but money always demands more of its suitor.

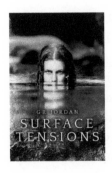

Surface Tensions (Island Adventures Book 1)
https://grjordan.com/product/surface-tensions
Mermaids sighted near a Scottish island. A town exploding in anger and distrust. And Donald's got to get the sexiest fish in town, back in the water.

"Surface Tensions" is the first story in a series of Island adventures from the pen of G R Jordan. If you love comic moments, cosy adventures and light fantasy action, then you'll love these tales with a twist. Get the book that amazon readers said, "perfectly captures life in the Scottish Hebrides" and that explores "human nature at its best and worst".

Something's stirring the water!